"I don't mess with marrie...

00695996

Jorja sank dow... muddled and ...

"But I'm not aski... you to—" Dan frowned his displeasure "—mess around. There's no reason for either of us to feel guilty about anything. There will be a divorce. It could come through within a matter of months unless—" he faltered "—unless spanners get tossed into the works."

"And if they do?" she asked.

"If Hilary withdraws her consent, then all hell will break loose." Dan scowled, and Jorja felt the urge to wrap her arms around him, to tell him she would make everything all right. But she didn't. Even if he was a free man, would she be wise to allow their relationship to develop? Dan's first marriage was no copybook example. Why should a second turn out better?

ELIZABETH OLDFIELD began writing professionally as a teenager after taking a mail order writing course, of all things. She later married a mining engineer, gave birth to a daughter and a son and happily put her writing career on hold. Her husband's work took them to Singapore for five years, where Elizabeth found romance novels and became hooked on the genre. Now she's a full-time writer in Scotland and has the best of both worlds—a rich family life and a career that fits the needs of her husband and children.

Books by Elizabeth Oldfield

Don't miss any of our special offers. Write to us at the following address for information on our newest releases.

Harlequin Reader Service
901 Fuhrmann Blvd., P.O. Box 1397, Buffalo, NY 14240
Canadian address: P.O. Box 603,
Fort Erie, Ont. L2A 5X3

ELIZABETH OLDFIELD

beware of married men

Harlequin Books

TORONTO • NEW YORK • LONDON
AMSTERDAM • PARIS • SYDNEY • HAMBURG
STOCKHOLM • ATHENS • TOKYO • MILAN

Harlequin Presents first edition September 1987
ISBN 0-373-11012-X

Original hardcover edition published in 1986
by Mills & Boon Limited

CHAPTER ONE

'I LOVE you,' Toby confided, plastering one, two, three energetic and decidedly jammy kisses on to her cheek. His chubby arms wound tighter. 'Do you love me?'

In grave danger of being starved of oxygen, Jorja attempted to ease his stranglehold.

'Yes, I do,' she gasped.

'How much?'

'Oodles and oodles!'

The little boy beamed his satisfaction. 'Do you love my grandpa?' he asked next.

The question drew a chuckle from the silver-haired widower currently occupying Jorja's desk. Mr Lecomber's attention might purport to be on papers which concerned a property sale clinched that morning, yet half an ear had been reserved for what was happening on the other side of the teak-panelled office. That was where his real interest lay. Jorja suspected that it would be rare if anything Toby said or did went unnoticed, for Thomas Lecomber had been sorely afflicted by the doting grandfather syndrome.

'Of course,' she grinned.

'How much?'

'Oodles and oodles.'

Toby beamed again, delighted that everything was proceeding to plan. He pushed his face closer. 'And do you love my daddy?' he demanded.

'Good grief, no! Not at all. Whatever made you

think that? It's your mummy who loves your daddy, not me. I'm just his assistant. We work together, but——'

Jorja brought herself up short. Whoa, girl! She was making an ass of herself, sounding sniffy and righteous like her mother. Toby had jerked back to gaze with huge round eyes, while Mr Lecomber's quizzical look asked why she had not simply carried on with the game. Why hadn't she? A glib pretence— yes, she also loved his daddy—would scarcely have sent a thunderbolt crashing down to split her asunder. Yet at the query an emotion with no recognisable name had crept out of the woodwork of her mind, leaving her unable to continue. No matter that she and Dan, her absent boss, shared a supremely innocent relationship, albeit a friendly one; stating allegiance to another woman's husband could not be sanctioned. Not in any form. What had happened in Australia last year guaranteed that.

'I like him,' she said, resolving to guard against being so heavy-handed in future.

'How much?'

'Oodles and oodles,' she vowed, and a grin from her rosy-cheeked inquisitor indicated that the situation had been retrieved. Jorja gestured towards a crescent of jam doughnut which lingered on a paper plate. 'I thought you were hungry?'

Assuring her that he was, Toby set about demolishing the remains, and had almost finished when the telephone rang. 'Me get it,' he carolled, splattering crumbs in all directions as he scrambled from her knee, but it was Mr Lecomber who answered the call.

'An enquiry about the Macclesfield estate,' he hissed, placing his hand over the mouthpiece. 'Keep

Sunny Jim quiet for a minute or two, will you?'

'Me not Sunny Jim, me——' started up an indignant treble, but the protest faded as Jorja fed the three-year old the final piece of doughnut and whisked him out of the office.

In the cloakroom she wiped his hands, washed all trace of raspberry jam from around his mouth, and brushed down his denim dungarees with their scarlet elephant motif. She also rinsed her own cheek and checked the state of her tightly belted sage-green dress. Despite Toby's mountaineering it had survived unscathed. Amazingly her tights were in one piece, too.

'No noise, remember?' she warned, a finger to her lips, but when the pair of them tiptoed back the telephone conversation had ended.

'That was the dairy farmer Bruce showed round a couple of days ago,' her elderly companion revealed, as his grandson reclaimed a clockwork car and began chasing round the carpet on all fours. 'Seems he was impressed and would like a second tour. Could you ask Bruce to arrange things?'

'He's out for the rest of today, but I'll make sure he's alerted first thing Monday,' Jorja promised, writing a reminder on her pad.

'Thanks.' Her capable tone had prompted a grin. 'I knew my instinct was right and you should be prised away from that playschool. Your natural habitat is the business world.'

'The playschool was only intended as a staging post,' she pointed out. 'I was lending a hand until Pauline found a permanent helper.'

'Fair enough, but wiping runny noses and clearing up after finger-painting sessions was a sinful waste of your talents. For the first time in years this office is operating smoothly while Dan's away, thanks to you. Before he left for Lanzarote he was saying how in three months you've worked miracles. In his opinion you're the——'

'Don't believe a word,' instructed a polished gravel voice, and they looked round to find the door being shouldered open. A tall man, tousled fair hair falling over his brow, was struggling in, hindered by a cargo of suitcase, briefcase and a plastic carrier bag holding bottles of duty-free liquor. A raincoat was slung over one arm.

'Daddy!' shrieked Toby, and hurtled forward. The newcomer grinned, rapidly abandoning his load in order to catch the tiny tornado and raise him aloft. 'Daddy, my daddy's come home,' the little boy chanted, smacking kisses willy-nilly on to a lean, tanned face.

Mr Lecomber watched benignly. 'Quite a welcome,' he commented, as he and Jorja shared a smile.

The reunion of man and child, both blond, grey-eyed and so clearly from the same stock, was heart-warming. Dan was returning kiss for kiss, rumpling the pale shiny hair, poking a finger into the plump tummy.

'What a noisy squidgebonks you are,' he teased, sending Toby off into a fit of the giggles.

'You've taken us by surprise, arriving back a day early,' Mr Lecomber remarked when the first flush of greetings had subsided, and his son was sprawled in a chair with the three-year-old fastened to his chest like a limpet.

'That's obvious, and while the cat's away——?' came the wry observation. Jorja received a lopsided smile. 'Maybe you do have a reputation for being super-efficient, Miss Reynolds, but your game's been rumbled. Now I know what happens the moment my back's turned—you entertain gentlemen of all ages!'

Her amber eyes sparkled. 'They've both been on their best behaviour. There's not been one spilt drink, nor has the furniture been wrecked.'

'Cuts no ice.' Mock-stern, Dan swung to his father. 'How come when Jonathan and I were kids the office was sacrosanct, yet this rapscallion—' the rapscallion in question had his tummy tickled '—gets a free run?'

Mr Lecomber gave an unrepentant shrug. 'He insisted it was high time he came and sat on Jorja's knee.'

'And me did!' Toby announced, sounding so triumphant that everyone laughed.

'Lucky you, but in five minutes Grandpa's taking you home, because your lady-love and I have things to attend to,' Dan informed him. 'It's called work.'

As the two men exchanged a few words about property matters, Jorja buttoned the little boy into his coat.

'Bye,' she said, giving him a cuddle and a kiss. 'See you again.'

'On Sunday? We go to the—' a finger was sucked, '—warwium?'

'The what?' asked Dan, his interruption telling her that, contrary to appearances, he had been listening.

'The Aquarium. Last weekend your father, Toby and I went to the zoo,' explained Jorja, straightening, 'but because it's so big we didn't manage to see everything.'

'And you're to pay a return visit?'

'Not me,' Jorja said hastily. 'I mean, there's no

need when you're here. I only joined in because Hilary was away, it was the nanny's day off, and Toby can be a handful for one person.'

'For an old dodderer like me,' Mr Lecomber elaborated cheerfully.

'Hilary'll still be away this Sunday,' Dan told her, and frowned. He slotted his fingers through thick fair hair, dragging back a cowlick which, seconds later, sprang forward to claim its original place across his brow. 'Why don't we both go along as extra support?' he suggested.

'I—I have something else fixed.'

'Another time, then.' Her employer became brisk. 'Don't wait dinner, Dad. I want to catch up on what's been happening over the past two weeks, and that could take forever.' He bent, squatting down to speak to Toby on his own level. 'As for you, squidgebonks, here's your goodnight kiss and I'll see you in the morning.'

'Me come in your bed,' the little boy promised happily.

'But not too early,' his grandfather warned, before turning to Jorja. He slid her a wink and said in a voice intended to carry, 'Thanks for the entertainment, and remember next time I'm the one who gets to sit on your knee.'

'No!' came the expected wail of protest. 'Me sit on Jorja's knee. *Me*!'

'Then I'll settle for a kiss now. Okay, Toby?'

There was a pout and a grudging, 'Okay.'

Grinning, Mr Lecomber tilted his head, and Jorja duly obliged.

When grandfather and grandson had departed, Dan went through to his own office and after about five minutes called Jorja in. Armed with a folder of outstanding correspondence, plus lists and notes of telephone calls, she was well able to alert him to the multitude of transactions which had taken place during his absence.

'Looks like business is rolling over well,' he commented half an hour later when she had completed her résumé. 'Nineteen properties sold and ten more which seem almost certain to go isn't bad for this time of year.' He raked through the pending correspondence and selected half a dozen letters. 'Think we could answer these now? It'd ease the load for Monday.'

The replies which Dan dictated kept her busy, and as the afternoon faded into evening Jorja was dimly aware of voices calling farewells in the general office along the corridor. Everything grew still. She was not a clock-watcher and didn't mind working late, but even so it was with a sigh of relief that she reeled the last letter from her typewriter. After preparing the envelope, she carried the completed pile through for signature. Her employer was on the point of uncapping his fountain pen when the telephone rang.

'Sorry,' he said with an apologetic smile, and the correspondence had to wait.

Leaving him to deal with the call, Jorja returned to her office. There she dimpled the venetian blind and peered out between white slats. The February evening was dark, wet and windy. Rain diagonals lashed across the windowpane. Below her last-minute shoppers joined office workers in a frantic chase along streets slicked to black glass. Heads bent and shoulders hunched against the rain's icy sting, homeward they scuttled, intent on reaching the warm and dry. Jorja knew she should be grateful she was warm and dry—the offices of Lecomber & Co., leading land and estate agents in the wealthy farming county of Cheshire, were a comfortable oasis in a prestigious city-centre precinct—yet battling with the outside elements suddenly struck her as preferable to being marooned here with Dan.

Why? she wondered, curling a lustrous strand of dark hair round her finger. The young managing director was not about to take advantage of their isolation, and pounce and paw. Acting the lecher was not his style. Indeed, hadn't a crucial factor in her agreeing to work for him been the knowledge of how he was respectable, upright, decent? From childhood, when he had been a 'big boy' on the periphery of her life, she had regarded him as a knight in white armour where personal qualities were concerned. It was true that since then adjustments had been required, when she had been forced to admit he could make mistakes like anyone else, but the conviction that her employer was Mr Integrity remained intact. Daniel Lecomber was no threat.

'These are for you, and I believe you have something for me?' intruded the polished gravel voice, and Jorja spun round, her complexion deepening from peach to rose when she saw that the object of her thoughts had walked in through the door connecting their offices. Whatever the weather outside, Dan invariably sloughed off his jacket and worked with shirtsleeves rolled up to the elbows. This evening his tie had been tugged loose and his collar unfastened, as if to emphasise that here was a man involved in accomplishing much in a minimum span of time. He slung the folder of signed mail on to her desk, slid his hands into his trouser pockets, and grinned. 'I'm waiting.'

'For what?'

Humorous grey eyes watched her move into action, separating the folder's contents into letters, envelopes, carbon copies.

'My kiss.'

'Your kiss?' she repeated.

Jorja kept her head down, her hands busy. Ever since Toby had said those six words, 'And do you love my daddy?' she had been edgy. Somehow the question had stripped off a layer of skin and left her feeling raw, over-sensitive. In consequence a kiss now took on the proportions of a loaded topic. She knew Dan's habit of saying things with his tongue lodged firmly in his cheek, she knew she should respond in kind, but easy camaraderie was hard won.

'Toby's had his and it's not two hours since I saw you press your luscious lips to my father's temple. They've had their quota. I'm here to collect mine.'

'Sorry, wrong age bracket,' she managed to quip, telling herself not to be an ass again. She must play it lightly, play it cool. That was all this was, *play*. Dan might be a knight in white armour, yet he was anything but dull. On the contrary, since coming to work at Lecomber & Co. she had discovered that he possessed a sneakily mischievous sense of fun. She folded a letter and inserted it in the relevant envelope. 'Union rules categorically state that in order to be entitled to my kisses Lecomber males must either be attending a pre-school playgroup three mornings a week, or have attained the age of sixty-five,' she continued.

'Which means that I'm to be discriminated

against?' A dark-blond brow lifted. 'Understand this, Miss Reynolds, my first act on Monday morning will be to send a strongly worded letter of complaint to my Member of Parliament. Deprivation of civil rights is not a matter to be ignored.'

'There is an alternative. You could be patient. Thirty-four years aren't that long to wait.'

'No?' For a moment his face clouded, and she had a fleeting sense of a two-tier conversation where words went blah-blah-blah and eye contact said something completely different. Just as she was beginning to feel agitated, Dan shrugged, and the atmosphere lifted to become light-hearted again. 'You could be right. If the next three decades pass as rapidly as the last I'll be hobbling round to draw my old age pension in no time at all.'

'It seems like only yesterday you were a gangly youth,' she grinned, able to relax.

Dan's absence had meant her workload over the past fortnight had been far heavier than usual. There had not been a spare moment. Now Jorja accepted that she would be functioning on her last reserves of adrenalin and was doubtless strung up a notch too high. This sensitivity, rawness, hint of undercurrent, was imagination brought on by fatigue.

'Built like a heron with my long thin legs, you mean? And doomed to trip over the size eleven feet stuck on the end of them. How I envied Jonathan! He was synchronised from his first step.'

'As graceful as a panther,' she agreed.

'There speaks another admirer!' The sigh he heaved was straight theatre. 'My brother may have been dead near enough four years, yet I'm still pestered with women stopping me in the street so they can reminisce about how wonderful he was, how dynamic, how sexy. And, believe it or not, they were all his discards.'

Jorja was alert to the implication. 'Like me?' she said, a smile flickering round the edges of her mouth.

A lift of shoulders stated agreement. 'Even though you were an extremely pretty eighteen-year-old, you weren't his type.'

'Not sophisticated enough?' she suggested, realising Dan must know little about that distant, short-lived episode.

'No way. But if Jonathan was around now he'd be making a play for you.' The clouded look of a few moments ago had returned. 'You've changed, Jorja. You're not an untuned piano any longer. You——'

'We've all changed,' she broke in. 'The clinical definition is "growing up". Speaking of which, Toby gets to be less a toddler and more a little boy each time I see him. He appears to add an inch a week. He's going to be tall, like you.'

'Another teenage heron.' Dan took a two-page report from her desk. 'Is this the spiel you've prepared on Mellor Lodge?'

Jorja nodded. 'It's ready for the brochure.' She waited as he scanned what she had written. 'Did I go over the top with my purple prose?'

'Shamefully.' His eyes sped down the page. ' "Original charm and character have been retained," ' he quoted. 'Which, in translation, must mean the place hasn't known a lick of paint for years.'

Jorja came to peer round his shoulder at the details.

' "Set in wholly unspoilt woodland", ' she read.

'Ten acres of rampant wilderness. Whoever does buy Mellor Lodge'll have to be someone who thrives on challenge.' Dan was at his sardonic best. 'Possessing more money than sense would also help.'

'The place has potential.' She had only been out to the half-timbered Georgian manor house once, yet had fallen halfway under its spell. 'Dilapidated, I grant you. But delightful—could be,' she amended when a downward turn of mouth indicated disbelief.

'Even with a glossy hand-out to provide that extra thrust, I reckon the Lodge'll be murder to shift. Get one of the boys to photograph the property from several angles before you finalise the brochure,' Dan instructed. 'Preferably angles which conceal any galloping dry rot.'

'Will do.'

Abruptly aware they were standing so close together that her shoulder was brushing against his arm, Jorja scampered back behind her desk. Touching Dan alarmed her. She realised she was being over-sensitive again, but she could not help it. Her composure, normally sturdy, had developed annoying jumps and twitches. Be sensible, she told herself. An element of physical contact exists in all working relationships; the graze of one hand on another when documents are exchanged, the neutral pat on the back, actions like that—they're nothing to get uptight about. But the operative word was 'neutral'. There lay a problem. Until Toby had voiced his question her employer had been securely labelled in her mind as nice, but neutral. Not any more. Instead suddenly, disturbingly, Daniel Lecomber had risen up as six-foot-two of clean-cut masculine virility.

'You're up to date now,' she said, adopting an air of conclusion.

'And you intend to depart?'

'Shouldn't I?' The words glimmered with rebellion, for he had appeared to administer a reproof. Jorja inspected the watch on her wrist. 'It's gone six, and after two weeks when at times it's felt as if I've been running the entire universe as a one-woman show, I reckon I'm entitled to go home.'

'Is Bruce wining and dining you tonight?' She shook her head. 'But I take it the two of you are getting together on Sunday? Bruce is the something else you have fixed?' Dan queried, handing back her own phrase.

'No. He's going down to Wiltshire for the weekend. He did suggest I join him, but——'

'At his parents' home?' came the interruption.

'That's right, but my mother's been pressurising me to stay with her, so I opted for that instead.'

Tanned arms were folded. 'Thank God at least one mother's interested in her offspring,' he muttered, then brooded for a moment as though the observation had released a flock of unwelcome thoughts. 'How is your mother?'

'Still nursing a jumbo-sized grudge. She slanders my father non-stop. To hear her speak he was the devil incarnate, *is* the devil incarnate.'

'Poor guy! Do you see him much these days?'

'I sneak down to the Cotswolds every couple of months, and I do mean sneak.' Jorja pulled a face. 'Once, without thinking, I mentioned I'd been to see Dad and Anne, and my mother almost went berserk. She demanded to know what possible attraction I could find in visiting 'that barmaid', as she calls her.'

Dan frowned. 'I thought your stepmother was an accountant?'

'She is, though a part-time one now, but she had a

spell serving behind the Golf Club bar—that's where she and my father first met. It was a one-off thing as a favour to the manager, but it provides my mother with the perfect opportunity to portray her as a bosomy blonde whose sole capabilities are pulling pints and pulling the fellows.'

'Your mother's feelings haven't mellowed with time?'

'Not a scrap. And she insists on heaping all the blame for the failure of her and Dad's marriage on to Anne. That man-eater, that stealer of husbands! She'd have Anne tarred and feathered if she could.'

A muscle moved in his jaw. 'Divorce is never easy.'

'Divorce is hell—always!'

'Sometimes it can be the only solution,' said Dan in a flat voice.

'Huh, try telling my mother that! She's made a cottage industry out of how an idyllic marriage was snaffled out from under her nose by a heartless floozy. Every time I see her, out come the same old accusations.'

'How did she react to you moving in with Pauline when you came back from abroad last autumn?'

'Badly!' Jorja's sigh held remembered despair. 'At first she came at me with protests, then switched to inducements. But I knew how, in the past, she'd lived her life through my father, and I was terrified in case she tried to hang herself like an albatross round my neck. I realise it sounds hard-hearted, but that was one reason why I left home four years ago. Mind you, my mother's far more independent these days. She's the leading light of a handicraft group and plays whist twice a week. She's made her own circle of friends. Before, anyone she knew she seemed to know by virtue of my father.'

'So your walking off into the sunset was a wise decision? Your mother's become self-sufficient and so have you.' Dan fixed her with a steady grey gaze. 'You matured while you were away, Jorja. Where there was a girl now there's a fullgrown woman.'

The effect of his eyes on hers jolted, and she discovered an urgency to retreat into business matters.

'Wasn't it great news about Hawley Brow? When the contract arrived, signed and sealed, your father and I couldn't stop smiling.'

He twitched his nose. 'I detected the heady aroma of triumph the moment I walked in through the door. The two of you appear to have set up a mutual admiration society, with Master Toby as an honorary member, of course. My God, they take their leave and it's hugs and kisses all the way!'

Kisses. Under cover of her laughter, Jorja's mind raced. She must steer clear of talk of kisses, find a diversion.

'What's the latest on the Lanzarote apartments?' she enquired. 'Are they as magnificent as Señor Cebrian prophesied?'

'They're good.' Dan clasped his hands behind his head and stretched, shoulder muscles gliding beneath the fine white cotton of his shirt. He looked tired, which was not surprising after two weeks in the company of the unreliable and voluble Lorenzo Cebrian. 'I wouldn't say they're the cross between New York's Plaza Hotel and the Hanging Gardens of Babylon which he described, but they're good all the same. As you know, there've been frequent occasions when I've longed to place my hands around Lorenzo's windpipe and squeeze, but I must admit he's finally come up trumps. I'm going back to Lanzarote next month, and you're coming with me.'

'Am I? Why?' she asked, as twitchy as if he had announced he intended she should jump from a high ledge.

'Because, being a red-blooded male, I relish the prospect of jetting off to an exotic location with a willowy brunette by my side.' The impudence of his grin only increased her twitchiness. 'Come mid-March there'll be two furnished apartments ready for show, and I'd like you there to take notes. Then you'll be in a position to wow prospective buyers with your purple prose. With competition fierce in the holiday and retirement apartment field, our advertising must make an immediate impact. The more titillating your descriptions, the more apartments we'll sell.'

'You hope.'

'I hope.'

'But there's no need to go to the expense of flying me out there,' Jorja protested. 'I can take whatever information I require from the files.'

He shook his head. 'It's not the same. Files don't give you the seaweed tang of the breeze, the orange sun setting behind squat whitewashed cottages, the luminous tranquillity of the ocean at dawn.'

'With descriptions like that, you could write the copy yourself!'

'No, thanks, that's your domain,' he decreed, a flick of the cat-o'-nine-tails in his voice. Although they had known each other for years, Dan was never afraid to remind her who was boss, and she respected him for that. 'In addition to writing your purple prose, I'd like your help with inventories and several other things,' he continued. 'The paperwork over there's badly in need of the touch of an efficient hand.'

Jorja took the soft option by allowing the matter to rest. Arguing had to be fraught with pitfalls. If he demanded that she spell out her objections to accompanying him to the Canary Islands, what could she say? That she had suddenly become aware of him as a male, with all the sexual connotations that implied? He would think she was crazy! Besides, shortly after Christmas she had accompanied him on a business trip to London, and his behaviour had been friendly, undemanding and totally proper as befitted a married man. Was there any reason to suppose a visit to Lanzarote would find him changed? None. With a wife like the beautiful Hilary, Dan was not about to stray. His needs, both emotional and physical, would be well catered for at home. No, any change was in *her*.

Jorja worked quickly, folding the remaining letters and sliding them into envelopes. The sooner she was out of the office, away from her employer, the sooner common sense would return. She licked the flaps with a moist pink tongue and pressed them down, then went to crouch at a filing cabinet.

'Could you spare a minute to give me more details on what's been happening with the Macclesfield estate?' Dan asked, looking on as she tucked the folder of carbon copies into a low drawer.

She stood, and with the brisk use of high-heeled shoe and shin propelled the drawer shut with a resounding thud. 'I can.' She hoped she didn't sound as reluctant as she felt.

Following him into his office, she noticed his limp was in evidence this evening—a leg injury resulting from the car crash which had killed his brother troubled him, and more so when he was tired. The past fortnight would have been strenuous. She knew he would have been constantly on the go, for whatever Daniel Lecomber undertook, he undertook it with enthusiasm. Standing back and looking was never enough. He would have been climbing round the hillside building site, with little consideration for his gimpy leg.

'As I mentioned, there've been several enquiries, though whether they're genuine or not is anyone's guess.' Jorja did a quick mental recap. 'The dairy farmer Bruce showed round is for real, because he wants a second look. Bruce also drove out a couple interested in opening a health hydro, plus he's had several conversations with a well-heeled newspaper owner who's looking for a country retreat.'

'Our Brucie appears to have been a busy little bee,' came the droll comment.

'He has,' she agreed earnestly. 'He's enjoying being back at Head Office where it all happens. He reckons the move's revitalised him.'

'Has it—or have you?' Dan dropped down into a brown leather chair and flung her a look which would have shattered concrete. 'I'm not paying the two of you to conduct a courtship when you should be damn well working.'

'That's not fair!' she retaliated, knocked on to the defensive. Not only did the man behind the desk look tired, he appeared to be under stress. Slumped back, he was chewing frantically at a thumbnail. 'We both work hard and you know it. And we're not conducting a courtship. We've only been going out together for six weeks or thereabouts, and it's very low key.'

'Couples meet and marry in less than six weeks,' snapped Dan.

'Couples might, I won't! After my parents' troubles I'm extremely cautious about matrimony.'

'So you've considered marrying Bruce?'

She glared. 'I have not! Don't put words into my mouth. What I meant was that I'm wary about marriage in general. I'd never rush into any commitment. After all, you go into marriage on the basis that you'll be married for life.'

'Do you?' He leant forward. 'Are you saying you haven't sized Bruce up as husband material?'

His derisory tone fuelled her temper. 'I'm saying don't be so nosy, and don't be so damned aggressive. You may pay my wages, but that doesn't give you the right to roar at me like—like a bull elephant!'

Jorja's chest was heaving, her amber eyes glittered. They had never fought before, so this squall was as surprising as it was stormy.

'Shouldn't it be like a heron?' he enquired, and his mouth quirked. The destruction of his thumbnail was abandoned. 'I apologise—I didn't mean to flare up. I don't know what's the matter with me lately. Maybe I'm in line for a cold?'

'Or maybe it's time you went home, put your feet up and had a stiff whisky or two?' she suggested, thankful that his anger had abated. The explosion was out of character. Dan kept his emotions under tight control, and was reliably even-tempered whatever frustrations arose in the day-to-day running of the business. She indicated the overflowing in-tray. 'Why not leave that? It'll still be there on Monday morning.'

'Tomorrow morning,' he corrected, fastening his

top button and pushing up the knot of his tie. 'You might not be on duty this Saturday, but I'll be here. However, you're talking sense.' Calm once more, he rose and strode across the tan-carpeted office to collect his jacket from the coat stand. He grinned at her over his shoulder. 'I notice Toby remains bewitched. The love affair's lasting well. What's that—nearly five months now? I remember the day he rushed in from playschool and announced that he'd met Jorja with the yellow eyes.' Dan thrust an arm down a sleeve. 'Little did he know history was repeating itself. You bewitched Jonathan with your yellow eyes,' he reminded her when she frowned.

'Not for five months I didn't!'

He laughed. 'True. Toby has more loyalty. Considering he's only three he's already showing——' Dan broke off. He had swivelled, taken a step forward, and his foot had become entangled amidst a loosely assembled coil of cord attaching a lamp to an electric socket. In an attempt to free himself he kicked at the cord, stumbled, and began to topple. Jorja catapulted forward, flinging herself against him to keep him upright. 'Still falling over my feet!' he joked, holding her in his arms in a way which had her wondering just who was saving whom.

'That cord's dangerous. On Monday I'll speak to the cleaner and——' The words dried up. Dan's pupils had dilated, and once again his eyes appeared to be saying things his vocal chords never had—or would. Jorja's heart pounded so hard she was certain he must hear it, feel the vibration. She ripped her hands from him, stepping back. 'I must go,' she blustered, and flew to the door with indecent haste.

CHAPTER TWO

WALKING along the path atop the city walls on Monday morning, Jorja found it difficult to prevent an idiot smile. Spring had put in an early appearance. The sky above was blue, and although a crispness demanded she wear her violet woollen cape, the sun was doing its best to raise the temperature. The day sparkled. She sparkled. It was impossible to quell her delight at simply being alive—and back home.

For Jorja, her birthplace held a unique magic. An architectural treasure-trove, evolving from Celtic settlement, via Roman fortress and seventeenth-century coaching stop, to modern-day county town, Chester was a joy to behold in all seasons, but especially in the spring. Interwoven with the quaint cobbled streets and famous black and white timbered houses were parks and shrubberies in plenty. Today snowdrops nodded tiny white heads amongst the grass, but soon daffodils would sing a golden chorus in the gardens of the ancient cathedral.

Jorja loved to walk the high stone walls. The two-mile circuit, punctuated by towered gateways which in bygone days had been equipped with portcullises and drawbridges, provided an excellent view of the bustling city streets within, while in the other direction lay glimpses of the green Cheshire plain. On her way to the office she passed many interesting sights; fine olde-worlde hostelries, the remains of a Roman amphitheatre, shops crammed with antiques.

25

A sense of satisfaction infused her, and that idiot smile rivalled the sun. This was where she belonged. Her place.

Friday evening had been analysed, rationalised and dismissed. Her fancies had simply been the result of three months of denying Daniel Lecomber any attraction whatsoever. A determination to erect the barrier she used with all married men had had her regarding him not so much neutral as downright neutered! He wasn't—far from it. Dan might maintain that Jonathan, flaxen-haired and dashing, had cornered the family's supply of sex appeal, but he was wrong. It was true that in their youth his brother had made all the running with the girls, yet although Dan had been thought by some to live in Jonathan's shadow, Jorja felt it had not been a case of subordinating himself, rather he had done his own thing in his own way. The younger of the Lecomber sons had been a late developer. At thirty-one, however, he had more than made up for lost time. Hadn't she ample evidence of how his female staff went marshmallowy whenever Daniel's crooked smile shone their way? He did not possess the flamboyant punch which his brother had packed, instead his appeal was subtle and seemed infinitely more compelling.

If she was a little susceptible, so what? There was no cause for alarm. *Liking* him was not a crime. On Friday, when she had abruptly recognised him as the charismatic man he was, Jorja had been knocked off balance. From swinging too far in one direction, she had swung too far in the other, overreacted. Her thoughts had slid into chaos, oddly fusing the present with the past. She had looked at Dan and picked up signals Mark had once sent. Faulty signals.

She ran down the flight of stone steps which led to street level, the heels of her grey leather boots rasping out her progress. All that swinging around in wild arcs had stopped. She was steady now, making sense. Over the weekend she had even gone so far as to accept that she was fond of her boss in a mild way. It was a fondness generated by shared memories, though somewhat tenuous and intermittent ones. As members of the same golf club, their fathers had first put them in touch. Not exactly *in touch*, she thought with a grin. Due to her mother's horror of those noisy, grubby, clumsy things called boys, their families had never socialised. But sometimes Dan had been in the back of his father's car, or she had seen him lying on the grass with his head in a book. He had just vaguely been around. She could not recall childhood conversations, probably because there hadn't been any. Seven years separated them, and teenage boys regard little girls as anathema. By the time she attained adolescence herself, Dan had lolloped off into his twenties, and the distance between them had seemed wider than ever. As she neared adulthood a blip of fate had resulted in Jonathan providing a point of contact, but only briefly. After that there had been a long gap, during which she had gone abroad and Dan had married, then on her return from Australia she had met Toby and the Reynolds-Lecomber link had been forged afresh. Yet the little boy's existence had come as a complete surprise.

'I didn't even know Daniel Lecomber was married, let alone had a child,' she had remarked to Pauline, when Toby had been identified.

'It all happened very quickly, must have been a few

months after you left,' said her friend, an auburn-headed girl with a generous figure. 'The wedding was a low-profile register office affair. Everyone wondered about the rush, but when Toby appeared and people could do their sums the reason became obvious. Dan married Hilary *after* he'd impregnated her.'

The snippet had been imparted as though it came from a file marked 'smutty secrets', and Jorja had felt a sudden chill. The besmirching of Dan, the affable clodhopper from her youth, was unwelcome.

'Seems odd he didn't take more care,' Pauline had mused, impervious to her discomfort, 'but if he was carried away on the spur of the moment you can't blame him. Hilary's delectable. She wears fantastic clothes, and she has the figure for them.' The redhead had smoothed a hand over a rounded thigh and grimaced. 'Still, I bet she needs to keep to a constant diet. She's a model. Must be in high demand, because she's off on foreign assignments two or three times a month.'

Jorja had raised her eyebrows. 'Sounds as if much of her time is spent away.'

'Not much, most.'

'I wonder why Dan doesn't put his foot down?'

Pauline had grinned. 'I understood marriage was a partnership, not a dictatorship?'

'Agreed, but what about Toby? Shouldn't Hilary be around for his sake?'

'There's a nanny, and Mr Lecomber's in regular attendance.'

'A child still needs its mother,' Jorja had insisted.

She hitched the strap of her leather bag higher on her shoulder. Since meeting his son, the link between her and Dan had been consolidated. Before Christmas his previous P.A. had given notice that she would be moving south with her husband, and the elderly Mr Lecomber had taken this as a signal to move into action. As a lobbyist he had been lethal. Each time he had delivered and collected his grandson from playschool, he had spouted his cause. Jorja would be perfect for the job; the job would be perfect for Jorja. One week she had been approached, the next persuaded, the third installed in her streamlined office. And throughout all this Dan had applauded.

It was entirely possible he also applauded his wife's dedication to her career. Because in her view a nanny and grandfather could never compensate for a mother, it didn't mean he felt that way too. Certainly Jorja had never heard him complain, but then mentions of his wife were rare. Her employer did not meld home life with business. On the one occasion when Hilary had put in an appearance he had grimly introduced them, then ushered her into his office, only to usher her out after a scant five minutes. Yet if he had been irritated by his wife's arrival in the middle of a busy afternoon, secretly Jorja had welcomed it. She had been longing to take a peep at Hilary Lecomber, and was not disappointed. Without boasting, Jorja accepted that she herself was attractive. A heart-shaped face, unusual amber-yellow eyes and a wealth of healthy brown hair which glinted copper in certain lights meant she received her share of compliments, yet in comparison she had felt a very plain Jane. Clad in a lavender suede skirt suit, and with long, long legs and a mane of shiny blonde hair, Hilary possessed the glamorous *whump!* of a pantomime prince. Wolf whistles and male cries of delight would be a constant accolade. Dan must count himself a lucky man to have scooped up such a prize.

Returning greetings and comments on the good weather, Jorja walked through the general office to her room. Here she shed her cape, tucked her grey silk blouse more neatly into the waistband of a grey and heather pencil-slim skirt, and set to work. Dealing with her share of the morning mail took time, for there was the usual gamut of interruptions to run. As the managing director's personal assistant—a job description which encompassed everything from secretarial work to dealing with clients and composing purple prose for the more important pieces of real estate on Lecomber & Co.'s books—her working day rarely flagged. When Dan was there they worked in unison. During his absences she filled the gap, and over the months had become skilled at oiling and meshing the various gears of his empire.

Two or three years previously Thomas Lecomber had relinquished his role as head of the firm. At first he had continued to work on a half-day basis, but in time those half-days had dwindled. Now his appearances were spasmodic, and he was expressing the intention to retire altogether. Bruce, a personable young man brought back from one of the outlying offices, was doing a good job of taking over what remained of Mr Lecomber's areas of interest, but sometimes he needed help. If Dan wasn't available, Jorja found she was expected to listen to his problems and make suggestions on how best to solve them. She seemed to give the impression of being far more in control than she felt, for in addition to Bruce regarding her as a helpmate, managers from the branch offices had also started to appeal for her aid.

Sometimes, however, they just wanted to talk, and she was jettisoning the phone after a particularly rambling conversation when a grey permed head poked round the door.

'Mr Thomas has rung to say both he and Dan'll be late in this morning,' reported Elsie, the plump matron who acted as part-time secretary to the elder Mr Lecomber. 'Dan has an unscheduled meeting with clients, but it's my guess Mr Thomas has decided he'll stay at home and play with Toby.'

'Could be,' grinned Jorja.

Thomas Lecomber's half-days had dwindled for one reason—his grandson. A previous heart attack and numerous doctor's warnings had failed to deter the widower, and he had stubbornly continued in his workaholic ways until one day a baby boy had smiled a toothless smile. As that baby boy grew into a charmer on fat legs and learned to grab for an earlobe and croon 'Ganpa', so Mr Lecomber's joy in extolling the virtues of houses for sale had seeped away. His life had taken on a new purpose, and now Toby's presence at the Old Vicarage, the family home, was a source of pleasure from morning until night. More and more the nanny who came in daily found herself playing gooseberry, while grandfather and grandson cavorted.

Elsie walked forward to shove a cutting beneath Jorja's nose.

'I've been showing this to the girls in the general office. My niece is working as an *au pair* in the South of France, and she sent it to me. Small world, isn't it?' she asked, and waited expectantly for an answer.

The cutting, a coloured photograph from a magazine, showed a group of men and women lounging by the side of a turquoise-blue swimming pool. With medallions glinting round their necks and a cigar or a drink in their hands, the men possessed an affluent air, while the women were from the Hollywood starlet mould.

'One of these is your niece?' queried Jorja, not understanding.

Elsie wheezed, laughter swelling her bosom. 'My word, no! They're your beautiful people. The pool's at some swanky hotel near Monte Carlo.' She pointed a finger. 'Don't you recognise the blonde in the tiny bikini, the one with all the hair? It's Hilary, your boss's wife,' she added, when Jorja looked blank.

'Is it? I've only met her once, and——'

Elsie's tongue made a tsking sound. 'Plain as daylight. My niece remembered seeing her driving through town in that open-top sports car of hers, and recognised her straight away.' Lowering her voice, she glanced furtively round. 'What I wonder is—does Dan know about this?'

'Is there anything to know?' countered Jorja. She had neither the time nor the stomach for Elsie's innuendoes. The woman had a fascination with other people's dirty laundry, and if it wasn't dirty showed no hesitation in manufacturing a few stains herself. She perpetually had a character assassination on the go. 'If this is Hilary, which seems doubtful because the picture isn't clear, she'll have been relaxing after work with friends. Seems perfectly reasonable to me.' She did not say 'and innocent', but that was implied. Jorja returned the cutting. 'Do you know if one of the boys'll be free later? I need someone to run me out to Mellor Lodge. Room dimensions must be checked for the brochure, and there are photographs to be taken.'

'You're out of luck.' Her snap showed Elsie was nettled; Jorja's lack of interest had been a let-down. The girls in the general office were in full agreement that yes, it *was* Hilary Lecomber and she must be up to no good. 'There's not a man in the place, they're all involved following up Saturday morning's enquiries. A couple of them should be back late afternoon, but that's about it. Bruce has disappeared for the day,' she added pointedly.

'I know. He called in for a word just before he left.'

At this point Elsie's role of procurer of all knowledge where the Lecomber employees were concerned came to the fore, and she elected to dismount from her high horse.

'Getting along well together?' she enquired, her omnipresent curiosity enshrined in a smile.

Jorja gave a noncommittal nod and, in order to avoid further questions, swerved into a grumble. 'I wish I could afford my own car, then I'd be able to drive out to Mellor Lodge myself.'

'Why not wait until Dan arrives and request a loan of his Mercedes?' came the half-joking suggestion. 'Lovely motor, that. He ran me home in it once when my back was playing up.' Elsie sighed. 'Lovely man, too.'

'How is your back these days?' asked Jorja, only to curse the question a moment later when her visitor perched comfortably on the corner of the desk.

'My doctor's amazed I can stand upright. He says in all his years he's never seen a spine like mine. The medical term is——'

The recital was long and involved. Jorja nodded, murmured, lost interest. Conscious of time being wasted, she shuffled her papers and gave meaningful looks at her notepad, but even so twenty minutes had passed before her message hit home and the woman departed. Head whirling with all there was to know about the idiosyncrasies of Elsie's backbone, she resumed work. Her concentration was such that when the connecting door swung open and she raised her head to find Dan standing there in a Donegal tweed sports jacket and dark trousers, she gazed at him like a dazed child.

'I am entitled to be here,' he grinned.

Jorja looked at her watch. It was long past noon. 'I know, it's just that——'

'Time passes so quickly when you're having fun?' He rested a shoulder against the door frame. 'Elsie tells me you require transport out to Mellor Lodge?'

'Yes, but it looks as though I'll have to wait until tomorrow.'

He shook his head. 'I'll drive you there and I'll take the photographs.'

'But the matter isn't urgent,' she protested, and to her confusion found she was blushing. 'You have more important things to do than go driving around the countryside. Shouldn't you deal with your in-tray? I've just added a fresh batch, and how about——'

'We're going today, now.'

'Now?' she bleated.

His beatific smile indicated that he viewed her consternation as amusing.

'I don't expect you to dance a jig for joy, but you needn't look as though placing yourself in my company means you're destined to wake up in ten hours' time drugged and naked in a harem,' he said, and her already hot cheeks grew hotter. 'After we've finished at Mellor Lodge, how about grabbing a bite to eat? There's an old pub not too far away which has a reputation for serving excellent bar lunches and real ale. I've been intending to give it a spin for ages.'

'Why not take Hilary?' Jorja suggested brightly, chattily, hopefully.

'In preference to you?'

'Er—yes.'

Dan gave her a long level look from between the kind of naturally lush lashes actresses would kill for. 'Because I don't choose to.'

If there was an answer to that, she could not think of it. Avoiding his eyes, she collected her cape and bag, and went out with him to the car. The city and suburbia were quickly left behind, and when they were driving along the narrow lanes he started to report on his meeting earlier in the day. Jorja's tension lessened. With the sun dappling the hedge-rows and buds beginning to show in the trees, the excursion took on the dimensions of a jaunt. Her companion was jaunty, too. He made her laugh, and by the time the Mercedes swung on to the flagged courtyard of Mellor Lodge the normal ease she felt with him had been restored.

'Psst! Wanna buy a load of trouble?' Dan asked from behind his hand as he unlocked the front door. 'Complete with woodworm in every beam and breathtaking examples of rising damp.'

'You're supposed to be positive about this place,' she protested.

'I am—positive it's a bad buy.'

'Not bad, just . . . doubtful.'

'Positively doubtful.' Their footsteps echoed as they walked across the dusty entrance hall, an area which Jorja had described as 'generously proportioned', but which now seemed like a barn. 'I hope the next owner has a fifty-piece collection of stuffed hippopotamuses to fill up the corners,' said Dan, with a sweep of laconic eyes.

'There's nothing wrong with wide open spaces.' She took a measure and notepad from her bag. 'If you want to go ahead with the photographs, I'll re-check the measurements.'

'What, and arrive back indoors to discover you've been gobbled up by deathwatch beetle?' He stamped a foot on the wood-blocked floor. 'At least this seems sound. Good surface condition, too. It'd be ideal for dancing.'

Jorja laughed. 'Listen to the expert! When did you last dance?'

'A long time ago,' he admitted, 'but I've had my moments. Don't forget you're looking at a guy who once jitterbugged for three hours non-stop on the back of a hay wagon.'

'And in the pouring rain,' she said, recalling a Rag Day procession in her youth when students had gone a little barmy, dressing up and parading to raise money for charity. She had been a schoolgirl spectator and Dan, then around twenty, had seemed very grown-up. 'I bet you can't jitterbug now,' she challenged.

'I bet I can.'

'Go on, then.' Jorja was taken by surprise when a long arm slid round her waist. 'On your own, I meant! I can't jitterbug, such things were before my time.'

'A likely tale!' He had become a pseudo-Groucho Marx with a most engaging leer. 'However, I shall teach you, my little passion flower. You'll find you can learn a lot from us older men.'

She laughed, her eyes shining. 'And what could I

possibly learn from you that I don't already know?

Dan twirled imaginary moustachioes. 'It's not so much the knowledge, my little passion flower, as the technique.'

'Poppycock! I'd wager my technique against yours any day of the week.'

'Done.'

The word fell like an auctioneer's hammer and Jorja's heart stopped beating. For some foolish reason, she and Dan had been flirting. That was bad enough, but now the flirtation had ended and something far worse, far more threatening, had taken its place. Forget Groucho Marx. The man with his arm round her was Daniel Lecomber, and he was looking at her in the same way as he had looked at her on Friday. The air became electric. She felt his intensity, knew imagination could not be held responsible for the yearning she saw in his eyes. She lurched back, breaking body contact.

'I must measure the rooms.'

'Stay,' he appealed. 'There's something——'

'Later.'

She flashed a giddy, white smile and turned, heading for the staircase and escape, but had not covered three yards before large hands landed on her shoulders. She froze. She attempted to shrug off his hold, but it was no use. Dan steered her around to face him.

'I want to talk to you.' His voice was low and serious.

'What about?' she demanded, fear clipping the words. How dare he lay his hands on her? How dare he abandon his jaunty air? Everything had been easy, *safe*, but now . . .

'The trouble I'm in.'

'What trouble?'

'My marriage.'

Jorja clasped fingers to her throat as a thousand conflicting feelings threatened to choke her. 'Dan, your private life is your concern, not mine,' she insisted.

'I need to talk.'

'Not to me.'

'*Yes*.' His eyes were burning like pale grey flares. 'From every side I hear how understanding you are, and——'

'You expect tea and sympathy?' she snapped. 'Sorry, you've come to the wrong person.'

He frowned, taken aback by her belligerence. 'I could use a friend,' he said heavily. 'You.'

'No!' She knew that somewhere there had to be a coherent and reasoned argument for her refusing to listen, for him to keep quiet, but sensible rebuttals refused to come. All she could do was shake her head until it threatened to come loose and repeat, 'No, Dan, no.'

'It's important I tell you what I feel.'

'It isn't !'

'It is.'

'Why?' she demanded.

'Because it concerns you and me.'

Jorja gazed at him in horror. How could he say 'you and me' with such a throb in his voice? How could he make it sound like a . . . coupling? Memories of Mark surfaced to intermingle with what was happening now.

'We're just colleagues in business harness,' she informed him, her tone as icy as the frozen wastes of the tundra. 'You and me don't exist.'

'Don't we?' There was a taut pause in which he left the question to dangle. 'I know I'm being premature, yet I can't afford to sit on the sidelines and watch you and Bruce become serious.'

'We aren't,' she objected. 'We won't.'

'If he's already reached the stage of asking you home to meet his parents, he must have plans.'

'You're wrong!.'

Dan grunted impatiently. 'You may think the two of you are, quote, just good friends, unquote, but I guarantee Bruce doesn't. That's why I daren't keep quiet, because if I do——' He made a savage pounce with his fingers. 'I can see no alternative but to tell you where it's at,' he said, with a bleak laugh at his Americanism.

'There isn't even an 'it', so it can't be *at* anywhere!' she blasted back. 'You have no right to talk like this to me. You happen to be married, or has that fact conveniently escaped your notice?'

'There's no love, never has been, between Hilary and me.'

'Go no further!' she ordered, jamming a hand up against the empty air. She had been betrayed. She had believed him to be constant and true, and here he was—tearing off that white armour to expose a murky outfit beneath. 'I've heard it all before. Your wife doesn't understand you?' she jibed, so brutally that he recoiled. 'Save me the clichés!'

'No clichés. Hilary understands me. She has me weighed up to the last ounce.' Dan pressed his lips together. 'It's you who doesn't understand, Jorja. This is confidential, but instead of flying straight to Lanzarote a fortnight ago I spent a couple of days holed up with a firm of solicitors in London, trying to hammer out a workable arrangement for a divorce. When a couple split, custody of any children is usually granted to the mother, but I'm adamant Toby must stay with me.'

'Why London solicitors?' she queried, drawn in against her will. 'Why not consult local ones?'

'Because then there'd be the danger of rumours, and I can't risk that. Hilary's volatile, she needs to be handled with care. She's screwed things up so many times in the past that before any package is set before her it must be watertight. I spent two full days with those solicitors; if I'd done that in Chester someone would have noticed—and talked.'

Jorja felt punch-drunk. 'Then I presume Hilary doesn't know you're taking steps to end your marriage?'

'She's aware I want a divorce—she should be, I've asked her for one so many times!—but she has no idea I've set the legalities in motion.'

'Why don't the pair of you consult a marriage guidance counsellor?'

'My God, how can you guide a marriage which never existed in the first place?'

'But this'll just be a bad patch,' she insisted, struggling to get to grips with what she had been told. 'You've not been married a full four years yet—give it a chance!'

'Those years seem like forty. And this isn't a bad patch, marrying Hilary was wrong from the word go. I only went through with it because—' Dan raked both hands through his thick fair hair '—because there were pressures. I feel as if I'm living in hell,

Jorja. That's why I'd be grateful for your moral support.'

His appeal thrust her back on to the defensive, and once again she remembered the past. 'Moral support today and *im*moral support tomorrow?' she derided. 'Isn't that the way it goes?'

His gaze narrowed. 'You think this is some devious method on my part to move in on you?'

'I think you might just be softening me up.' She glared. 'Couldn't "friend" be a euphemism for "a little bit on the side"?'

'Don't be so goddamned cynical! You're acting as if I'm the enemy, which I'm not. You must know me well enough to realise I'd never——'

'Never?' she taunted, chin held high.

'Jorja,' he warned, 'cut out the nastiness.'

'Who's nasty? It merely crossed my mind that the idea of our going to bed together might appeal.'

Dan did not flinch. 'It does—very much. Look, I have the feeling I'm banging my head against a brick wall here. Give me the measure, and we'll get to work.'

At last allowed to climb out of the snake pit, Jorja took advantage with a speed akin to frenzy. She marched him through one empty echoing room after another, checking and rechecking dimensions. The final room they measured was the master bedroom. Here Dan leant a knee on the mahogany window-seat and rubbed clean a diamond pane in the casement window. He squinted down at the sunlit lawn, then turned to scan the lily-papered walls.

'Now this room docs have potential. Can't you imagine a four-poster in here? Preferably one with a deep feather mattress where you could laze in voluptuous comfort?'

Jorja eyed him dubiously. 'What about the panoramic views?' she asked, remembering what she had written. 'You could wake up each morning and watch your ponies galloping round the far paddock.'

'I'd rather wake up each morning and gallop round that four-poster after you. Yes,' he added, when she stiffened, 'that's what I'm expected to say, isn't it? How come I've been classed as a sleazy two-timer when I've never made a single advance, never even attempted to kiss you?' He regarded her with cold grey eyes. 'I'm a fool. I see now I've been indulging in some very sloppy thinking. I'd imagined you might have been prepared to listen, maybe give me some back-up, but it's obvious I've misjudged you. I'll take the photographs, then we'll head for the office. That pub lunch doesn't seem so palatable any more.' He strode across the room. 'Forget what's been said here today,' he instructed from the doorway. 'You want everything to be strictly business between us?' He gave a mocking bow. 'Lady, it shall be as you wish.'

CHAPTER THREE

DAN meant what he said. In the time it took to drive back to the office he built an invisible wall between them, and during the days which followed made it plain he had no intention of allowing access to whatever might be going on behind the brickwork. The strange thing was that the other members of his staff did not appear to notice this tightening in his attitude. They acted as though he was the same old Dan. He wasn't, and Jorja found it increasingly difficult to respond. He was not unpleasant, indeed, he was immaculately inoffensive. He was so careful, so courteous, that sometimes she wanted to scream. Instead of being grateful for his propriety, grateful he had withdrawn as requested, she was stricken by a bewildering sense of loss. Restlessness overtook her, and she did not understand why.

'It's my belief that what matters most in this life is the family,' pronounced Thomas Lecomber, two weeks later. His hair, like his son's, possessed a mind of its own, and he brushed a silver wing from his brow. 'Families give you the best times, but also the worst.'

Jorja knew he was remembering Jonathan, for a flicker of subdued but recognisable pain crossed his face. Yet, despite the pain, he drew comfort from reminiscing about his elder son, that golden boy whose love of speed had brought his life to an abrupt end at the age of thirty. Of late his reminiscences had

43

increased. Almost as if to make amends for Dan's strict adherence to business, Mr Lecomber had become garrulous. Whenever he visited the office he would buttonhole her, and talk and talk and talk.

'I hear the bad times are supposed to be—what's that newfangled expression?—growth experiences ,' he continued, steepling his fingers and gazing into the middle distance. 'Damned hard way to grow, if you ask me. And have you ever known anyone suddenly become a saint because life gave them a nasty poke in the eye?'

A reply was not expected, and as he ambled off into his nostalgia Jorja found herself wondering what Dan would have been like if his brother had not been killed. Different, yes, but not much different. Dan was his own man. He—— She snipped off the thought and instead gave herself a ticking off. Her employer was out of the office this morning, so why not use the opportunity to keep him out of her head? He had been under consideration far too often recently. Yet keeping him out of her head was impossible, because Mr Lecomber had now brought him into his musings.

'From babyhood my sons were opposites,' he told Jorja. 'Dan was sociable, but equally happy with his own company. Jonathan needed to be in a crowd, and leading that crowd. Dan was drawn to reading, music, matters of the mind, whereas Jonathan shone on the sports field. I still have the athletics trophies he won. I wonder if Toby'll win trophies one day?'

Jorja had never been able to decide whether or not Jonathan had pride of place as the favourite son. He was always spoken of in glowing terms, yet perhaps it was a case of Mr Lecomber remembering only what he wished to remember? Certainly the old man's relationship with Dan was strong and true. He was content that Dan had taken over the reins at Lecomber & Co. when barely into his thirties, but she wondered if he would have been similarly content if his elder son had taken charge. Admittedly, Jonathan would have made a dazzling front man with his heart-throb good looks and charm, but dazzle has its limitations. In her opinion Dan was hard to beat where business acumen and spot-on decisions were concerned.

But was her opinion valid? Jorja gave an inward shrug. There seemed a distinct possibility it might not be. One of the qualities she would have said Dan possessed, as opposed to his brother, was staying power. What had happened to that staying power now? After four short years of marriage he was arranging a divorce. So he said. But could his talk of divorce be counterfeit? He had told her in confidence—wasn't that a standard married man's ploy? My wife and I are splitting up next week, next month, next year. And in the meantime, baby, how about you and me interlocking? Jorja went cold inside. It was a hackneyed scenario. She did not want to believe Dan was a selfish seducer, but she had been misled before.

Her opinion leapfrogged. On the assumption that he had been telling her the truth, with Hilary so often away maybe his marriage did not seem to be worth much, yet there was Toby to consider. An intermittent mother must be preferable to no mother at all, so why couldn't Dan persevere and find a way of working through this current crisis? Why didn't he attempt to coax Hilary back into the family fold? Whatever he said—she was doubting him again!—he must have loved the blonde once upon a time, and urgently. She could have imagined Jonathan discarding a wife, but never Dan. Jorja frowned. She had been wrong about his staying power; what else was she wrong about? In her youth the differences between Jonathan's and Dan's personalities, temperaments and style had seemed clear-cut; now she wondered whether Dan might have more in common with his brother than she had ever imagined.

Mr Lecomber focused on her again. 'When you and Dan are in Lanzarote, will you do me a favour? Try and persuade him to take time off to unwind. He's living through a difficult period and——' The old man sighed, smoothing his fingertips along the edge of the desk. 'His marriage was at my insistence,' he muttered, as if talking to himself. 'What else could I do? Toby makes it worthwhile, Dan agrees with me on that, but——' There was a moment of silence. 'Where were we?'

'You were explaining about the latest development in the Hawley Brow deal. How a query's cropped up over a public footpath which cuts across one corner.'

'I remember.' Mr Lecomber's interest in business matters was rekindled. 'When Bruce comes in I'd like him to read up the details and go to see the new owners. There's no need for panic if he handles this sensibly. All that's needed is a little co-operation. Mmm,' he said, muttering again. 'That's what Dan needs from Hilary, a little co-operation.'

'This office is like a railway station,' Jorja complained the same afternoon. 'People rush in, people rush out, and you can never keep track of anyone. Your father wanted Bruce to go and see the Hawley Brow people, but he hasn't appeared. He was supposed to be in at two, and now it's well after three.'

Dan continued reading through a draft letter she had prepared.

'Bruce'll turn up,' he said vaguely. 'Is my father still around?'

'He went off before lunch.'

'Gone to feed the ducks?'

'More than likely.'

He shot her a glance. 'Don't sound so disapproving! Feeding ducks isn't a mortal sin.'

'I know. It's just that your father's supposed to be handing his responsibilities over to Bruce, but the two of them are never here at the same time, and guess who gets lumbered with passing on messages?'

'You,' he said, continuing to read. 'Is this mutiny in the ranks?'

'*Yes*,' she announced, so defiantly that he raised his head and grinned. To her bewilderment, Jorja discovered the curve of his mouth was compelling, and she grinned as well. 'If your father organised his time better it'd make things easier,' she tacked on, unwilling to be so easily disarmed.

The wall Dan had built still existed, but he had begun to allow himself the occasional relaxed smile, a joky observation. This was a relief. The sooner things reverted to normal, the better. But what was normal? Deep down she suspected too much had been said for them ever to return to the ingenuous rapport they had shared a little over a fortnight ago.

'Don't forget he's smitten with his grandson,' Dan replied, 'and when you're smitten all rhyme and reason fly out of the window. You must know what being smitten is like?'

'Maybe.'

'Only maybe?'

His grin had widened, and it struck her that this afternoon they were more relaxed with each other than they had been in a long time. Dan's grin lubricated the atmosphere, allowing her to answer in the same flippant vein.

'I've been smitten once or twice. When I was fourteen I carried a torch for Calum O'Connell, remember him? The boy who delivered fresh cream on a Saturday morning.'

'Not that skinny little runt whose hair hung down over his eyes like an Old English sheepdog?' asked Dan in surprise.

'The same. And you can't talk! I seem to remember you were pretty skinny yourself once.'

He flexed a forearm. 'That was before I sent away for my bodybuilding course. Now I'd give Sylvester Stallone a run for his money.'

'You think so?'

'Don't you?' he laughed. 'Tell me about Calum.'

'Well, with his pale skin and big dark eyes I found him terribly romantic. He was my idea of Chopin. I imagined him playing the piano in a maroon velvet jacket with a floppy bow at the neck, and all the while tragically expiring from consumption. I was amazed when he continued to knock at the door Saturday after Saturday. I caught sight of him in Eastgate Street last week.'

'And?' Dan asked, when she chuckled.

'He's as fat as butter, and has one of those desperate hairstyles where all the hair from one side of the head is swept over to the other in an attempt to conceal a naked scalp.'

'Not exactly a baldness full of grandeur, to quote

some poet or other?'

'More a baldness full of lacquer!'

They were laughing together when the door was flung open and a blonde vision in white leather appeared on the threshold. The laughter ceased, as if cut off by a knife. There was a moment of deafening silence, then Dan spoke.

'What do you want, Hilary?'

His wife swept a cool, assessing look over the pair of them which, for some unknown reason, made Jorja feel guilty. It was as if she and Dan had been caught *in flagrante delicto*. Her cheeks began to burn. She was certain Hilary noticed, for there was a split second's hesitation before she gave an arch smile and strode towards her husband as if staking a claim. In blouson top, skintight trousers and spindly-heeled boots, the blonde would have drawn all eyes in any crowd. A fox fur jacket was swept from her shoulders and tossed on to a chair in passing. Rounding the corner of his desk, she halted. She pushed both hands beneath the mass of golden hair, lifting it pin-up-girl fashion, and stretched. It didn't matter that the pose was artificial, for the impact of the leonine head, the glossed pouty mouth, the slender arc of her body, stunned the senses. No one said a word.

As the third which made up the crowd, Jorja felt awkward. 'I'll go,' she offered, wanting to leave.

'Stay!' Dan rapped out the command. He switched his eyes to his wife. 'I take it you're parading through the office to give the peasants the pleasure of drooling over your new clothes?'

Hilary allowed the blonde mane to fall. 'I finished my shopping earlier than expected and I'm thirsty. I thought maybe I could persuade you to offer me a drink?' She leant forward to stroke a cyclamen-coloured nail down his cheek. 'Please, Daniel.'

He remained immobile, the teasing touch being neither accepted nor rejected. 'What'll you have—tea or coffee? Or would a glass of hot milk be more to your taste?'

'Don't tease!' Hilary pouted prettily. 'You know the kind of drink I mean.'

'Sorry, I don't dispense alcohol at three-thirty in the afternoon.'

'Not even for me?' murmured his wife, playing little girl lost for all she was worth.

Jorja wished she had been able to make that earlier exit. Sitting here and watching Hilary go through her paces was giving rise to a distinctly uncomfortable feeling. Whatever kind of relationship existed between her employer and his wife, it was not a simple one. She sensed his temper was being curbed—barely. She also knew the blonde was play-acting, yet how far did the acting go? Dan had maintained there was no love between them, yet the arched body, the tantalising fingernail on his jaw, had been a definite come-on. Hilary considered her husband to be a highly desirable male, of that Jorja was certain. Those big blue eyes had a hungry look. If Dan's divorce talk had been genuine, and if he had now advised Hilary of the steps he was taking to secure his freedom, wasn't there a ten to one chance she had resisted? According to him his wife had not been receptive to the idea in the past, so why should cut and dried legalities now meet with her approval? Jorja frowned. The situation was confusing. She did not know what to think.

'Especially not for you,' Dan replied, levering his

long body from the chair. 'And if you have no further requests, Jorja and I have work to do.'

'Whatever it was the two of you were engaged in when I came through the door, it wasn't what I'd call work,' grated his wife, changing tactics. She placed her hands on her hips, the manicured talons a red shriek against the white leather. 'It doesn't take much imagination to deduce what goes on here!'

'So Jorja and I indulge in an orgy every afternoon?' he drawled. 'So what's new?'

'Do you intend to indulge in a daily orgy when the two of you fly off to Lanzarote next week? Yes, my love, I know all about that,' Hilary was purring, full of malice. 'Your father let it slip. He appears to imagine there'll be a chance for some relaxation between times.' Indolently she swivelled to Jorja. 'What will you be providing—a relieving massage for the work-worn executive?'

'You can retract that.' Dan's voice sliced like a razor.

'I do, I do,' she trilled. 'I'm sure Jorja knows I was joking, even if your sense of humour's off duty this afternoon.' She tripped back across the office, and was in the process of gathering up her fur when a knock at the door made her pause. 'Not another woman arriving to pander to your every whim?' she enquired scornfully.

Dan ignored the remark. 'Come in,' he called, and Bruce entered to find three pairs of eyes trained on him.

'I'm intruding,' he said awkwardly. 'I'll come back later.'

Dan found an easy smile from somewhere. 'You're not intruding at all. What can I do for you?'

'It's about this footpath at Hawley Brow.'

The mood broke. The air stopped jangling. With a twitch of her white leather hips, Hilary departed. Jorja felt drained. Nervous tension had kept her upright and alert during the blonde's visit, but now her energy was depleted. As the two men talked, the last few minutes re-ran themselves in her head like a private video.

Seeing Hilary a second time had prompted a reappraisal. Agreed she was delectable, yet didn't she veer towards the flashy? Her appearance had yelled 'look at me!' and her behaviour had been more strident orchid than shy violet. If asked to describe the woman in three words, Jorja would have chosen superficial, shallow and self-centred. All of which made Dan's original attraction difficult to understand. She would have credited him with more intelligence. Jorja gnawed at her lip. She was being naïive. Intelligence would not have come into it, urgent animal need would have swept all other considerations away. And if Daniel Lecomber did not seem the kind of man to be poleaxed by a glamour girl—what did she really know about him? Not much, it seemed. Three months ago, even two weeks past, she would have firmly pigeonholed him in the 'steady family man' slot. Yet that family man was intent on wrenching his family apart!

'Has one been made?' repeated Bruce, and she jerked herself from her semi-stupor.

'I beg your pardon?'

'Has an appointment been made for me to see the Hawley Brow people?'

'You don't need one. Mr Thomas has arranged for you to be able to see them any time, without notice.

He was hoping you'd go along this afternoon.'

'Then I will,' he promised, with a smile.

'Are you and Brucie boy still seeing each other?' Dan enquired, when the young man had gone.

'Off and on.'

He lifted the draft letter and subjected it to a studied concentration. 'With an emphasis on the on?'

'On the off,' she replied, wondering why she found it difficult to feel much enthusiasm for the tall, dark bachelor. Pauline rated Bruce as 'dishy', and she supposed he was. Pauline also vowed him to be the ideal mate, and her friend could be right there, too. Yet since the rise and fall of Dan in her life, the young man had seemed increasingly bland. The previous evening they had gone out to dinner. She had enjoyed the outing, thought what a pleasant companion he was, but had still been reluctant to commit to another date this week.

'Could you change the wording here?' Dan was scribbling an alteration in his big black scrawl.

'I'd rather not come to Lanzarote,' she blurted out.

'Why, because of what Hilary said?' He discarded pen and letter, to rest his chin on his hand. Like her, he appeared to have found his wife's visit enervating. 'Pay no attention. Because she's open to anything, she believes everyone else is equally suspect.' He gave a thin smile. 'A couple of weeks back I told you everything was strictly business where you and I are concerned, and it still is. There's no reason to ditch Lanzarote.'

'But Hilary——'

'To hell with Hilary! Everything that woman does is calculated to create an effect. Take the damned lovey-dovey routine she insists on using with me, for example. There's no intimacy between us, but because she sees herself as the ultimate in *femmes fatales* she has this compulsion to make people imagine something exists. It would be a boost for her ego if she could convince the world I'm besotted.' Dan gave a terse laugh. 'What a dent her ego'd receive if it leaked out that I never have been besotted!'

'I'd still prefer it if you went to Lanzarote without me,' Jorja said doggedly, blocking out this reference to his marriage.

'Sorry, but I won't have Hilary scaring you off. Why should she dictate your actions, our actions? If I want you there to help me, then help me you will. You're coming Jorja.' He found the draft letter again and took hold of his pen. 'There's just one paragraph on page three which——'

The springlike days of February seemed like a mirage. The weather had done a capricious about-turn. Leaden skies hung low over the airport, rime-frosted runways were silver-white, noses and fingers were nipped by the cold.

But the crowds in the departure lounge did not care. Present vagaries of the climate were of little interest. They were anticipating the sun which lay a few reachable hours ahead. Holiday fever hummed, and when the stewardess announced boarding instructions for the Lanzarote flight the travellers surged forward, bright in summer-style cottons.

Dan's outfit of T-shirt, jeans and sports shoes, a black leather jacket slung over his shoulders, was geared for the sunshine too. When he had picked Jorja up from the flat—with Pauline smiling in the background—a double-take had been required. Jorja was so used to seeing him in darkly formal attire, even if his jacket was mostly shucked off, that to find him laid back and casual unsettled her. His mood was also laid back and casual. Bricks appeared to be toppling off that wall, one after another.

'I trust you've brought lashings of bikinis?' he teased, as they waited in line.

'Just bowler hat and pin-striped suit,' she replied, her tone a little tarter than was necessary. 'This *is* a business trip.'

'All the way,' he assured her, but despite her own more tailored appearance in a cream overdress, with copper silk blouse beneath, she was beset with the disturbing image of them simply going off on holiday like their fellow passengers.

Pauline's attitude the previous evening had not helped.

'Aren't you the lucky one?' she had giggled. 'Flying off to the sun with Daniel Lecomber! That limp of his always makes me want to rush over and suggest he leans on me, *hard*.' The redhead had rolled her eyes. 'Oh, what I'd give for a dirty few days with him, all expenses paid! Just kidding,' she had added, stemming Jorja's rush of protest.

This was not a dirty few days. Nor was she on hand to help relax the work-worn executive, as Hilary had suggested. Not that Dan was work-worn. Watching as he stretched to place their hand luggage in the overhead locker, Jorja decided he brimmed with good health and vitality. Good humour too, for he smiled as the stewardess squeezed past him in the aisle, receiving a megawatt smile in return. Jorja noticed it was not a programmed, 'You're the customer and it's my duty to be pleasant' smile. More of a, 'You're cute,

and if you'd like to get to know me better I'm willing'
kind of reaction.

Perhaps he would like to get to know the
stewardess—or some other girl—better? They were to
spend four days in Lanzarote, but no law said they
had to spend them constantly together. Maybe on one
of those days, or nights, Dan would choose to go off on
his own? If his marriage provided no comfort, could
he be blamed for wanting the balm of soft arms
around him, a body interlocking with his? Jorja
plunked herself down in her seat. For a moment those
arms, that interlocking body had metamorphosed
into hers.

Seat-belts were buckled, morning papers distribut-
ed, the safety procedure enacted. Although she was
not frightened of flying, Jorja admitted to a nervous-
ness which all her travels had done nothing to dispel.
She braced herself for take-off, and yet when the
plane soared up through the sullen clouds and into the
blue and gold world which lay above, she felt an
unaccountable wave of pleasure. Was holiday fever
also affecting her? New places, new people were
always stimulating, and the prospect of four days on a
sunbaked isle in the Atlantic Ocean made her smile.

'Happy?' Dan was grinning.

'Yes, I am.'

Her reply was straight from the heart, and
uncomplicated. For the first time in weeks, her
emotions were uncomplicated. She was going to
Lanzarote with no strings attached. She and Dan
would work together, play platonically a little
together if he wished—and that was that.

CHAPTER FOUR

As the three hundred or so volcanoes which dapple Lanzarote's surface had once done, Arrecife airport seemed in danger of giving an inward rumble and suddenly erupting. Too small to accommodate what had in recent years become a deluge of sun-hungry visitors, the airport did its best, but almost an hour passed by before they managed to retrieve their luggage and wend their way through the jostling crowds out towards the concourse. Dan had quoted spring temperatures in the Canaries as being warm, though precisely how warm had not sunk in. Blowing a strand of dark hair from the clamminess of her brow, Jorja struggled to keep pace. Her companion had taken charge of their suitcases, but she still needed to cope with two travel bags, her shoulder bag, and a bundle of magazines which were threatening to cascade from beneath her arm. They were enough.

'It's hot,' she mumbled, catching up.

He grinned over his shoulder. 'What did you expect? We are only sixty miles from Africa.'

Outside there was a breeze. It cooled her skin and lifted coppery-brown tendrils from her shoulders. Jorja regained her calm, while in contrast Dan began to lose his.

'Typical!' he complained, fractiously pacing up and down. 'Lorenzo's never on time.'

The motor coaches which stood against the perimeter fence were moving off one by one, ferrying

57

holidaymakers to the hotels and apartments which were dotted around the tiny island. Hire cars were being signed for and driven away. People Jorja recognised from their flight were disappearing inside taxis, and still they waited.

'At last!' sighed Dan, when a thickset character in his late forties beetled into view. 'Don't squeal *too* loudly when he pinches your bottom!'

Lorenzo Cebrian did not pinch her, though it was a close run thing. Until that moment their contact had been restricted to a few telephone calls, yet he fell on her like a long-lost lover. True he flung a *'Buenos días'* in Dan's general direction and gave him a fake punch on the biceps while introductions were being made, but then he was smiling a wide, wide smile, looking deep into her eyes, gurgling compliments in an impassioned mix of Spanish and English. 'Pressing the flesh' took on a dramatically new meaning, for her hand was held and stroked as tenderly as if it had been a newborn kitten.

'I presume there's transport for us somewhere?' Dan enquired, impatient in his role of bystander.

Grudgingly Lorenzo redirected his attention. 'I've arranged a renta-car as you requested,' he said, the rrr's rolling from his lips like barrels down a hillside. 'Alas, it is ordinary. Had I known the lovely Miss Reynolds was to grace our shores, I would have arranged something grander.' His hand sketched what was presumably a Rolls-Royce, then moved into a serpentine gesture. 'Come this way, please.'

'Why didn't you tell him I was coming?' Jorja whispered, as they followed the Spaniard across the car park. Over the past week Dan had made several phone calls to Lanzarote, so she had automatically assumed Señor Cebrian had been notified about her visit.

'Because he gets high at the sight of a feminine ankle. If he'd known you were accompanying me he'd have laid on flamenco dancers, serenading violins, the whole caboodle. We'd never have done any work.' Sardonically he viewed the stocky figure in the flowered shirt and white trousers. 'What d'you bet he's already planning a few treats?'

'Your renta-car,' their escort announced, flashing an imaginary matador's cape when they reached a canvas-topped Suzuki. 'I trust you will find it comfortable, Miss Reynolds.'

'Please call me Jorja.'

'Jorja. Such a pretty name for such a pretty creature,' he breathed, and once more launched into a concerto of compliments.

'Jorja will take the room booked for me at the Hotel Camino, while I use one of the show apartments,' Dan informed him, cutting across the Latin grandiloquence. He had stowed their luggage in the rear of the four-wheel-drive, and was ready to go. 'That way I'll be able to check such things as the plumbing. You did assure me yesterday they were furnished down to the last teaspoon,' he rasped, irritated because the Spaniard's face had fallen. 'If there's been yet another example of *mañana* and the damn apartments aren't ready, I——'

'No, no, the show apartments are complete,' he was assured. 'The beds are made up, the kitchens equipped, but——'

'But what?' groaned Dan, wondering what could have gone wrong now.

As a veteran participant in Señor Cebrian's erratic

business methods, he had learned to detect a problem at fifty paces. During the eighteen months it had taken for the apartment community to be constructed, many promises had been made and many broken. Deadlines had been extended, bypassed, had disappeared into the mists of time. How much of the hassle he could attribute to the Latin temperament, how much to a breakdown in communications, how much to sheer incompetence, Dan had never been able to work out. The apartments were a quality scheme, and he supposed 'all's well that ends well', but he had had to push every inch of the way. At times he felt as if he'd laid every damn brick, plastered every damn wall himself. And even if Lecomber & Co. did have a financial interest, and were the sole agents handling sales in the U.K., acting as a goad was not a part of his remit. Now this final visit should have been straightforward. After dealing with one or two loose ends, he had expected to return home secure in the knowledge that he could confidently promote the development. But the look on Lorenzo's face warned of yet another catastrophe.

The Spaniard lifted wall-to-wall shoulders. 'Yesterday the telephone went cracka, cracka. I no understand. There has been a mix-up. It is life, you know?'

'No, I don't know,' Dan replied, using a voice which would have stripped paint.

'I thought you said you wished to occupy an apartment, so I cancelled your reservation at the Hotel Camino.'

'You cancelled! But I never said a word about where I intended to stay. Neither did I hear any crackle.'

A flush crept up Lorenzo's neck. 'It must have been

at this end of the line.'

'I bet!' Dan folded his arms. 'Well, you'll have to uncancel, smartish.'

'How?' Dark eyes rolled in meteoric despair. 'The Hotel Camino is fully booked. All the hotels are fully booked. There is not one spare bed on the entire island.'

'Great!'

'Ah, but do not panic.' Lorenzo stabbed at a solution with the verve of a picador stabbing a bull. 'Remember, two apartments have been furnished. You can use one and Miss Reynolds—Jorja,' he murmured, smiling at her, 'Jorja can use the other.'

'That suits me,' she said quickly, eager to restore Dan's soaring blood pressure to a more acceptable level. 'It'll give me an opportunity to write my purple prose from the insider's point of view.'

'You'll be able to enthuse over the siting of the broom cupboard and describe the egg cups in superlatives?' he suggested, tight-lipped.

'Something like that.'

'Okay, we'll take up residence,' he told Lorenzo, after a long moment of reluctance. 'I'd like to see you at the site office tomorrow morning at nine o'clock. Nine a.m., which doesn't mean nine-thirty, neither does it mean ten. Nine on the dot. Got it?'

'Got it,' the Spaniard agreed, chirpy now he had been let off the hook. 'I am at your service, *señor*.'

'Good, because the plan'll need to be gone through one last time, just to make sure you've not built an extra apartment or missed one out,' Dan inserted, but the comment went over the other man's head. 'I require details of final numbering, road names, etc. Where inventories are concerned, Jorja'll need to know what's been lined up for each different size and style of property, and——'

By the time he had finished listing tasks for the following day, Lorenzo's chirpiness had faded into shell-shock. Jorja doubted whether he had absorbed all the instructions. If by a miracle he had, she was convinced at least half had been put on 'hold', to be attended to at some vague date in the future. Hard work did not appear to have a high rating on the Spaniard's list of priorities, and proof of that came the moment Dan stopped talking.

'This evening you will both join me at the finest seafood restaurant on the island,' Lorenzo declared, disregarding the apartments and jumping into his own particular ball game. Beside her, Jorja heard Dan clench his teeth in frustration. 'There will be a choice of *mariscos*, *pulpitos*, *gambas* and many many fishes. Everything you eat will be a treat from King Neptune!'

'We can't make it this evening.' Dan was steely. 'We've had a lot of travelling, and an early night's called for.'

'Tomorrow?'

'No.' He frowned, then managed to squeeze out, 'I dare say we could come along on Friday.'

'Your last night? That will be perfect.' The extravagant rrr's were rolling around again. 'We will make the evening a celebration. My brother is owner of the restaurant, and the chef.' Lorenzo gave the information as though it was a remarkable coincidence. He placed his hand on Jorja'a arm. 'He will be thrilled when I tell him such a lovely young lady is to dine at his establishment. His heart will sing, his chest swell with pride!'

'And when this poor sucker pays the bill, his bank balance'll swell, too,' muttered Dan in an undertone.

In addition to being work-shy and a lover of the ladies, Señor Cebrian was tightfisted, notoriously so. This had had its advantages in the construction of the apartment complex, for he kept to a strict budget and abhorred wasting money, but Jorja had heard tales of how his hospitality—which meant a visit to his brother's restaurant—invariably resulted in his guests having to reach for their wallets.

'I'll see you at nine o'clock in the morning,' Lorenzo promised, as he handed over the keys for the show apartments. He kissed Jorja's hand, lingering over it in fond farewell, then headed off to claim his own car.

'I hope you didn't mind my refusing the invitation for this evening,' Dan said as they climbed into the Suzuki, 'but I was so bloody annoyed about his cancelling the hotel reservation I knew there was no way I'd be able to sit through a meal and smile nicely.' He adjusted the seat to give him room for his long legs, then fiddled with the wing mirror. 'I'd stake my life someone's been crossing Lorenzo's palm with silver. Money has to be at the root of his deciding to risk my wrath by offloading the hotel room in such a cavalier fashion.'

Jorja's brow furrowed. 'But how would he benefit?'

'Because I visit the island on a regular basis I pay a negotiated off-season rate which holds good throughout the year,' he explained. 'However, this being a peak period, my room could be rented out at twice the price. Split the difference between Lorenzo and the booking clerk, and——' He wafted a hand.

'Cynic!'

'Could be, but whenever our fat Spanish friend

smiles that sugar-coated smile of his, I always grow suspicious. If he can find a way to make the extra *peseta*, he will. I dread to think how much he managed to salt away while the apartments were being built.' Dan switched on the ignition. 'Let's hope I can remember to drive on the wrong side of the road.'

They left the airport and headed south, taking a road which maintained a haphazard parallel with the coast. As the plane had come in to land Jorja had noticed that, although there were patches of green, much of the island's surface seemed bare and was now interested to examine the terrain at close quarters. To their left the land dipped down to a shimmering counterpane of sunlit sea, while to their right there was a barren plain where faded black and red mountains formed an impressive backdrop. There were no trees, no hedges, no wild flowers—just miles and miles of gravel waste which reminded her of a moonscape.

'Lanzarote rose up from the sea through a process of eruptions,' Dan told her, 'and like all the Canary Islands has its share of volcanoes and black beaches.'

'Are any of the volcanoes active?'

'I believe there's the occasional murmur.'

'So by tomorrow morning we could be up to our necks in molten lava?' she grinned.

'I hope not! Who's going to want to sink their savings into an apartment where the view's pumice, pumice and more pumice? No, the last major eruption was in 1824, though the granddaddy of them all happened way back in the seventeen-thirties. Then thirty craters exploded simultaneously and spewed out sufficient liquid rock to totally change the face of the island. In places the rock layer was nearly forty

feet thick.' He lifted a hand from the wheel to indicate
a distant square of green. 'Incredibly, all was not lost.
Man's perseverance has been such that these days
Lanzarote grows vast quantities of onions, tomatoes,
melons. It even exports its own wine.'

'They manage to grow grapes here?' Jorja queried
in surprise.

He nodded. 'The vines are planted in mini-craters
and protected from the wind and the sun by lava
walls. The end result is a delicious Malmsey wine. I've
no doubt Lorenzo'll be plying us with it on Friday,
and raking in ten per cent!'

A few minutes later they reached a patchwork of
fields where lines of bright green onion tufts grew
from the dark cinders. A mile or two further, and the
road ran through a sleepy whitewashed village. An
old man was sitting on a bench dozing, his dog beside
him, but they were the only signs of life. Presumably
people did live, love and laugh behind the painted
shutters which were at present closed to protect the
houses from the sun's glare, but they had better things
to do than sit and watch the tourists go by. Yet Jorja
and Dan were not tourists. Why was it becoming
harder and harder to remember that?

'We're nearly there,' he murmured as they rounded
a bend, and Jorja took special notice.

A sandy bay stretched out before them. Rising up
from the beach, the hillside at first levelled off to
accommodate the road. No longer a bleak metalled
strip, it had become an attractive promenade where
geraniums and pink-white periwinkles grew in tubs
set at intervals on the wide pavements. Along the
promenade were cafés, and outside these holiday-
makers were clustered round tables, relaxing and

enjoying the scene. And interspersed with the cafés were boutiques and bistros, gift shops packed with leather goods, sunhats and shells. Higher still on the hillside bloomed spanking-white villas and apartments, arranged like daisy petals round azure eyes of swimming pools.

'Which is our development?' enquired Jorja, eager for her first glimpse.

'Our?' Dan teased, with a smile.

Although she had come in at the tail end of the scheme, Jorja had heard him chew over the trials and tribulations so many times she felt as if she had a vested interest. There were three hundred and sixty dwellings, cleverly situated around gardens and courtyards. She had read how flights of shallow steps connected the various levels, how there were six tennis courts, a club house and an in-complex supermarket. She knew all the statistics off by heart, yet when Dan pointed and said, 'There's *our* development,' she was unprepared for the size and sheer elegance.

White-walled and orange-roofed in traditional hacienda style, the apartments curved into the natural contour of the land. They drove in between granite gateposts, passed the cabin which served as site office, and headed up the hill. In the still heat of the afternoon came the noise of hammering, and a workman whistled as he slapped paint on to a wall, but the major proportion of the work had been done. Most of the dwellings were finished and waiting. There was an air of expectancy, as though people were hovering just out of sight, poised to rush in and fill the complex with the hustle and bustle of sunshine living.

'Very classy,' praised Jorja, as they drew to a halt beside a board inscribed 'Show Apartment'. She climbed out of the car and gazed around. 'I notice everyone gets a sea view.'

'That's a standard requirement. Likewise a balcony, plus bottles of cheap Spanish vino in the fridge.'

'The good life.' Below, in the distance, yachts bobbed on a bright blue ocean, children danced in the waves, sun-worshippers soaked up their daily dose on striped beach mattresses. 'You ought to bring Toby here, he'd love it. He could build sandcastles and paddle all day long.'

'It's the ideal place for families,' Dan agreed, and began to unload their cases.

Families. Did a little boy, his father and grandfather constitute a family? she wondered, waiting to collect her share of the bags. No. A proper family needed a wife, a mother, as its focal point. Hilary Lecomber was not providing that focal point. Difficult as it was to understand how any woman with a drop of maternal feeling could turn her back on a bubbly, open-hearted child like Toby, facts were facts: Hilary chose to spend more time away from her son than with him. And only last week Mr Lecomber had mentioned how her absences were stretching. At best her relationship with Toby had to be scrappy, for whenever he came into the office it was noticeable that he made no reference to his mother. It was also noticeable how he made a beeline for Jorja's knee, demanding hugs and kisses and assurances of her devotion. Her throat tightened. A degree in psychology was not needed to know that, despite the love his father and grandfather showered on him, the little boy felt deprived.

Maybe a divorce was the answer? Yet was there to be a divorce? Jorja was back where she started—racked with doubts. Frowning, she picked up their hand luggage and followed Dan into the apartment.

'Looks good, doesn't it?' he smiled, depositing her suitcase in one of the bedrooms. Hand-split cedar had been used in conjunction with pastels, and if the handsome tobacco and white décor of this room was anything to go by, the remainder of the accommodation promised to be a delight.

'Very good,' she affirmed. 'I can't wait to explore.'

'Let me drop my gear off next door, then I'll join you.'

Dan vanished, but before she had time to finish admiring the quilted bedspread and matching curtains, he had returned. 'There's been another of Lorenzo's famous mix-ups. I was under the impression the two furnished apartments were next door to each other, but I was wrong.' He juggled the bunch of keys. 'This is number 56. The tag for the other says 230. Heaven knows where that is. Give me a few minutes while I scout around.'

'I'll come with you,' Jorja offered. 'I'd like to get the feel of the place.'

As it seemed simpler to walk than take the car, they set off on foot. They had no luck in the immediate vicinity, and on going further afield soon discovered that the layout of the complex had much in common with a catacomb. An added problem was identification. While some porches did sport black numerals, others where workmen were *in situ* remained bare. Dan did his utmost to remember what he could from the site plan, but concluded the original numbering had undergone a vast change. Queries in his halting

Spanish drew a blank. For well over half an hour they tramped, passing empty swimming pools, deserted tennis courts, the splendid terraced club house, yet Apartment 230 remained elusive.

'Got the feel of the place?' Dan enquired drily.

'Just about,' she gasped, as they plodded up another incline between another range of apartments.

Gold and blush-rose were beginning to fill the sky, yet although evening was approaching the sun had lost none of its heat. Dan's T-shirt was clinging damply to his back, and he had begun to limp. With each of her own strides requiring more of an effort than the last, Jorja was not surprised. She was on the point of suggesting they should head all the way back to the site office and search for information there, when she spotted a board painted with the magic words—Show Apartment.

'There it is!' she exclaimed.

'Trust Lorenzo to come up with the bright idea of separating the two apartments by at least half a mile as the crow flies, and what feels like seventeen if you walk,' Dan said scathingly.

'Does it matter? At least this way prospective buyers have a chance to get——'

'The feel of the place?' His voice was thick with disdain. 'Yes, it does matter. I don't give a damn about prospective buyers right now, what concerns me is the thought of you being isolated on a building site all night. If we'd been within shouting distance that would have been something but the mileage between apartments 56 and 230 means you could be set upon by a horde of Apaches and I'd be none the wiser.'

'The apartments'll be Red Indian-proof. I won't

come to any harm,' Jorja replied, her words tinged
with exasperation. She was hot, sweaty and tired.
Problems were the last thing she needed. And here he
was, making a fuss about nothing!

'I disagree. Ghost town developments attract
sightseers by day and opportunists by night. There's
always some Joe, or in this case some Pedro, looking
to lift a bag of cement or a handful of nails, and if a
furnished apartment exists, why not nosy round and
see what can be filched from there?' Dan shook his
head, his jaw a bedrock of firmness. 'I'm not leaving
you alone with me so far away. I'll go and find you a
hotel room.'

'What's the point in setting off on a fruitless trek?'
she sighed.

'How do you know it'd be fruitless?'

'Lorenzo said there wasn't any accommodation.'

'Lorenzo exaggerates.'

'Does he? You saw for yourself how one plane after
another was landing at the airport, all packed to the
gunnels. Hotel rooms have to be scarce.' Seeing his
hesitation, Jorja kept on talking. 'Chasing around
trying to track down a free one isn't going to be
exactly fun, and I don't see any reason why we can't
both use the same apartment. There are two
bedrooms and—and I don't mind sharing if you
don't,' she finished up quickly.

'Aren't you worried about your reputation?' A
barbed-wire look raked over her. 'I do happen to be
married, or has that fact conveniently escaped your
notice?'

She recognised the recital of her own words as a
deliberate blow below the belt, yet refused to react.
The weary edge to his walk worried her. Dan had

been on the go since dawn, and now the sun was setting. It had been a long day.

'I'm offering a solution,' she said coolly. 'However, if you prefer to tour the island in the hope of stashing me away in a hotel for the night, that's your prerogative.'

His T-shirt had come adrift from his jeans, and he became very involved in pushing it back down.

'Okay.' He was terse. 'Tonight we'll share Apartment 56. Tomorrow I may decide otherwise.'

The rebuff made Jorja smart. Need he make it so obvious he did not want to be left alone with her? For a man who had once made a plea that she be his friend, he had become remarkably standoffish. Grief, anyone would think she was a raving nymphomaniac, about to back him into a corner with a whip and a chair! Her suggestion of sharing had been intended to make life easier for him—and this was the thanks she got! Whirling on her heel, she set off back down the hill as though wearing seven-league boots. Beside her Dan kept pace, but she did not spare him a glance. If his leg hurt, that was his problem.

Back at the apartment, Jorja adopted a nonchalant air. She toured the rooms with him, made all the right noises of admiration, then retired to her room to unpack. In less than five minutes her clothes had been stored in the wardrobe, her toiletries laid out in the en suite bathroom. What did she do next? She was damned if she was going to waltz out and make polite conversation, not yet. She would rest on the bed for a while, and maybe then . . .

When a knock on the door awoke her, it was dark.

'Supper's ready,' Dan called.

'Supper?' Bleary-eyed, Jorja attempted to come

alert. 'Oh, thanks.'

She washed quickly, changed into pale lemon slacks and a filmy batwing top, brushed her hair and went to find him. He was waiting on the red-tiled balcony, where a table had been set for two. Her eyes widened when she saw cold meats, fish and a bowl of green salad sat on the chequered cloth. Fruit, cheese and crusty bread had also been provided.

'I took the chance you'd be happy to eat in tonight, and went to a store a couple of miles along the coast,' Dan explained. 'I stocked us up with basics.'

'Looks a lot more than basics,' she smiled, her previous grumbles with him forgotten.

'Glad you approve. Shall we have a drink before we eat? What would you like? There's dry white and red wine, or I could rustle up a Sangria.'

'Sangria, please.' Jorja waited as he prepared the fruity punch, then laughed when he handed her the glass. 'You're very domesticated!'

'Aren't I just? Play your cards right and maybe I can be persuaded to make my speciality, Chicken Madras. Given the ingredients, I can knock the whole thing up in less than an hour.' Dan poured himself some red wine. 'Drawback is, it takes two days' hard labour to clear up the kitchen afterwards.'

'Then I'll pass,' she said smartly.

He fixed her with grave grey eyes and—click—she felt his mood change. 'I thought you might,' he muttered. He rested an elbow on the wide metal rail and gazed up into the sky as though counting the stars one by one. 'I told Hilary I'd consulted a solicitor,' he said quietly.

The evening was warm, but Jorja shivered. She had understood there would be no more talk about his divorce, but it seemed he had only been marking time.

'Oh.'

'You're supposed to say "Pass" to that, too,' he retorted, swinging round to confront her. 'Though I guess "Oh" will do nicely. It does convey the same iron shutters slamming down. I realise you must have caught the sharp end when your parents separated, but is that any reason to—' he spat out the word '—ostracise me? I can't help being in the same lamentable position.'

'I'm not ostracising you, and I didn't catch the sharp end. I was almost an adult when my father found the impetus to cut loose, and frankly it came as a relief. He and my mother had been making each other's lives a misery for years.'

Dan strafed her with a look. 'Then if you're not carrying a chip on your shoulder, what is it? Why won't you listen to me?'

'I——' she began, wondering if she dared admit to the humiliation of what had taken place in Australia, but he wasn't listening.

'Why the big rejection whenever I step one inch beyond what you consider's legit in our relationship? And we *do* have a relationship, one with magnificent potential.'

'I work for you, that's all,' Jorja insisted, as the ogre of their interlocking arose again.

'It isn't all. You must have a very short memory if you've forgotten how comfortable we were together a month or so ago. And that comfort was, to borrow someone's lyrics, the start of something big.'

'It wasn't !'

'No?' Dan gazed out into the darkness. The entire

sweep of the bay could be seen from the balcony, silver and black in the moonlight, while below, on the promenade, street lights formed a necklace of yellow diamonds. When he began to speak again, it was as though he was reading out a thesis. 'I distrust those instant heat-in-the-groin, ripping-off-your-clothes kind of affairs,' he said. 'If an attraction's rooted purely in the physical, then sooner or later you're going to wake up one morning and have to face the fact that, no matter how spectacular the lovemaking might be, it isn't enough. After that everything goes downhill, fast.'

'Does it?' she asked, deciding he must be referring to what had happened between himself and Hilary.

'It does,' he replied sternly. 'Couples need things in common, they must be able to talk to each other. You and I can talk, hence that comfortable feeling. We share the same background, laugh at the same things, we jell.' Dan swallowed a mouthful of wine. 'But we've been given a bonus. On top of it all there's a strong sexual buzz.'

'No!' Aware of squeaking, Jorja whipped her voice into control. 'If I appeal it's because you're feeling lonely and—and you've become disenchanted with Hilary and I appear to be her opposite. I'm dark, she's fair. I'm tall, she's petite. She's a high-flier, while even though I've travelled I'm basically a home-town girl.'

'She's flat-chested, and you have two comely handfuls?' he derided rapaciously, his eyes swooping down to her breasts. 'Talk sense, Jorja. And talk two-way. This isn't just you appealing to me. I also appeal to you. I have it on good authority that you like me.'

He gave his familiar lopsided grin. 'Oodles and oodles!'

How could she deny the truth? Yes, she did like Daniel Lecomber. She liked the way he moved through the world with unruffled ease. She liked the way his hair persisted in falling across his brow in golden threads. She liked his tall, rangy frame, his thickly-lashed grey eyes, his nose. In fact, she liked almost everything about him. Okay, maybe they were compatible, but a sexual buzz did not enter into the scheme of things. Could not enter. Must not enter.

'I do like you,' she admitted, 'but——'

'Forget the buts,' he murmured, and removed the glass from her fingers, setting it down on the table with his own.

Instinctively she knew he was going to kiss her, and the blood rushed to her head. She must stop him, but how? Jorja felt hypnotised. It was as if his will had taken control of hers, for as Dan looked down, his eyes moving to her mouth, so she was gazing up at him, enamoured by the curve of his lips. When he put his arms round her and bent his head an excitement, so all-consuming it was unlike anything she had ever felt before, swept over her. She was incapable of movement and barely of thought. His lips brushed across hers like a butterfly, and she quivered. Every nerve in her body was aware of him, of his closeness, of his maleness, of the freshness of his breath warm against her skin. His arms tightened, and mouth to mouth they were clinging. They seemed to be fused— chest to breast, thighs to thighs, legs against legs. Dan was firm-fleshed, his body lean and muscled. As they kissed his desire grew, and she felt him become hard against her.

With a tremendous effort she found the strength to wrench free. 'You mustn't. We mustn't,' she protested. Spots of hot pink were on her cheeks, her hair was tumbling into her eyes. 'Dan, you're married!'

'So I'm forbidden to kiss you? I know.' He took a deep steadying breath. 'Don't worry, it won't happen again, but I needed to prove——'

'You've proved nothing,' she cut in, desperate to backtrack, to obliterate, to deny. She wished her voice wouldn't wobble. Her knees were in danger of wobbling, too.

'On the contrary, I've proved everything. A fire's smouldering between us, just waiting to spring into flame.' His smile was tender. 'When we do get into bed I suggest we make sure an extinguisher's handy to damp down the sheets.'

'We're not going to get into bed!'

Dan shrugged. 'Not now, but——'

'Not ever! Never!' She was squeaking again.

'Never is a very long time. But if I did undress you and lie naked with you now, you'd give yourself to me, Jorja. You're as eager for me as I am for you. If I entered you I'd find you moist and warm and——'

'Dan!' she implored. She could not allow him to talk that way. It was too evocative, too exciting. She gulped in a breath. 'I don't mess around with married men.'

'I know. I respect that. But I'm not asking you to—' the flare of his nostrils showed deep displeasure with the phrase '—mess around. Trust me when I say there's no reason for either of us to feel guilty about anything. Shall we eat? Not each other,' he added, when she gazed at him. 'Our supper.'

With a mute nod, Jorja sank down on her chair. She

was muddled and confused, and most of the blame lay with the traitorous response of her body. She had been aroused, very much so. Even with Mark she could not remember feeling such an overwhelming need. Mark. As always the memory of her Australian lover made her shrivel up inside. But remember him she must. If nothing else could be salvaged from that shameful period of her life, at least she could use it to protect herself from making the same mistake twice. Dan. Mark. Granted there were differences between the two men, but weren't there also similarities? In silence she helped herself to the food her companion offered, in silence she began to eat.

'How—how did Hilary take the news about your consulting a solicitor?' asked Jorja, telling herself she was not so much *interested* as making a polite enquiry.

'Calmly. She said she was willing for me to go ahead, but——' Dan sighed. 'As I spoke I could see her mind ticking over. If she's given her consent it's only because at this moment in time it suits her. Next week things might change.'

'So a divorce is . . . doubtful?'

'It's Hilary who's doubtful. A divorce will take place eventually.'

The similarities between the man across the table and the man she had known in Australia merged, forcing out an exclamation.

'Ha!'

Dan's eyes narrowed. 'You think I'm spinning you a line, don't you?' he demanded.

A determination to learn from the past meant she must tackle matters head-on. 'You do appear to be covering yourself for in case nothing happens,' she replied, meeting the scorching intensity of his look.

'I'm telling the truth. There will be a divorce. It's possible it could come through within a matter of months unless—' he faltered '—unless spanners get tossed into the works.'

'And if they do?'

'Who knows?' He shovelled some meat into his mouth and chewed savagely. 'If Hilary withdraws her consent, which I have to admit is a possibility right up until the day the divorce is finalised, then all hell could break loose. You see, she has Toby as her supreme bargaining weapon. I've warned my father not to allow him out of his sight while I'm away, but——'

Her fork stopped in mid-air. 'You think she might spirit him off somewhere?' asked Jorja, aghast.

'I don't know what she'll do. All I know is that she'll use this divorce to advance her own ends.'

'Would Hilary want to raise a child by herself?'

'She'd hate it. My God, she finds more than five minutes in his company a chore!' Dan sighed. 'Even so, that wouldn't stop her taking possession and using Toby as a pawn.'

'Which means you'd have no option but to fight her in court?'

He nodded grimly. 'And as our marriage isn't one of the straightforward variety, any legal battle would be bloody and lengthy. That's not another line,' Dan growled.

'I didn't think it was.'

Jorja had now accepted that his talk of divorce was sincere, yet from her point of view did it really make much difference? She took another piece of the crusty bread. Consulting a solicitor was aeons away from being a free man, and even if he was, would she be wise to allow their relationship to develop? Whatever Dan's personal appeal, whatever compatibility or sexual buzz, common sense had to mark him down as a bad risk. His first marriage was no copybook example, why should a second turn out better? She hated herself for jumping ahead and being so coldbloodedly analytical, but as her mother had once said, maliciously predicting Anne's downfall, statistics show that second marriages are even more likely to founder than first ones.

'The success of any divorce hinges on Hilary feeling she's a drop-out mother, not a pushed-out one,' Dan pondered, pursuing his own line of thought. 'How can I make that happen?'

'I don't know.' She set down her knife and fork. Her plate was clean. 'Thanks, that was delicious. Do you have any idea if they smoke the fish locally? Perhaps I could take some home? Smoked fish is one of Pauline's favourite dishes.'

'Not only don't you know, you don't *want* to know,' he interrupted, a bite in his voice. 'Maybe this time you're not hissing and hollering because I've stuck my neck out and asked for help, but that's the message which is coming through loud and clear. God! I can't approach my father because he has so many hang-ups about his part in my damn marriage, and once again you turn me down flat. Never mind, I dare say I'll struggle through—alone!'

He scowled, reminding her so much of Toby in a rare, sulky moment that her heart turned over. Jorja felt the urge to wrap her arms round this moody man, and kiss him and tell him she would make everything all right. But she couldn't. She daren't.

'If I'm turning you down, it's because I must. Because——' her tongue came out to moisten too-dry lips '—because I have a responsibility towards myself, Dan. I'm not prepared to be dragged into the middle of——'

'I'm not dragging you into anything!' he blasted. 'You think I'd be dumb enough to put you in a position where Hilary could cite you as a co-respondent or something? No way. I don't intend you to be involved, and if we keep our heads there's no reason why you should be.' He moved uneasily, as if fretting beneath a heavy burden. 'All I'm asking is that you listen to me sometimes. Lend a shoulder to cry on. I want you in my life, but not physically. I'm lying. Yes, I do want you physically. Denying what I feel for you is like denying the force of gravity.'

'Four years ago you wanted Hilary, and what happened? You changed your mind.' Jorja saw him glower, but refused to be deflected. For her own protection it was essential that she be forthright. 'You could change your mind about wanting me.'

'Never!' Dan declared with harsh resonance. 'By five minutes past nine on the very first day you came to work for me I knew how right you were, how right *we* were, and three months together have only confirmed that feeling.' He rubbed his fingers across his jaw, growing pensive. 'Maybe the pull between us goes back much further?'

'You're fantasising,' she said impatiently.

'No. I'm not saying we were attracted as kids, but even when you were a schoolgirl——'

'An untuned piano?' asked Jorja, with a splash of vinegar. This was evasion. Whatever his feelings for her, the crucial issue was the relatively short time it had taken him to realise that despite his vows he was not prepared to remain with Hilary 'till death us do part'.

'Yes, even then I was aware of you.'

'Dan, four years ago you wanted Hilary. That's what we're talking about.'

He shook his head. 'No, no, I didn't want her.'

'So Toby's conception was the product of complete indifference?' Jorja demanded, irritated by this blanket denial of attraction to the beautiful blonde. She would not have given him a standing ovation if he had confessed to a heat-in-the-groin attraction which had gone downhill fast, but she would have applauded his honesty.

'Toby's conception was the product of lust on the one side and an eye for the main chance on the other.' He paused, a shadow crossing his face, then said with aggression, 'My marriage has been a marriage in name only.'

'Yes?' Seeing that red fingernail slide slowly down his jaw, Jorja could not keep from sounding sceptical. Flashy or not, Hilary possessed a many-splendoured appeal.

'It's been a sham, and a shambles. Now I'm attempting to right matters with the least possible pain to those involved. It won't be easy, because although Hilary's going along with the divorce right now I can't rely on her not to turn hostile.'

'She'd be extremely hostile if she thought you had another woman waiting in the wings.'

'She would,' he agreed. 'In reality she doesn't care a

toss about me, but she'd be furious if the public impression was of her being eased out to make room for someone else.'

'She isn't being eased out, at least not for me,' Jorja said hastily.

All of a sudden the night seemed to go very still, as if the tick of time had been halted. In silence they looked at each other.

'Then—then you won't consider waiting for me?' Dan asked, his voice gritty with anguish.

A pulse throbbed in his temple. Seeing it, Jorja yearned to reach out her fingers and soothe and comfort.

'No,' she said quietly.

'God, why can't we live in a properly ordered universe, one where this kind of situation would never occur? Then I'd be single, like you. I'd be able to pay court correctly.' He kicked back his chair and strode to the balcony. 'But it's not like that.'

After a moment, she rose and walked towards him.

'Dan, you can't ask me to live in a vacuum for an unspecified period on the offchance that some day you'll be free.' These were not recriminations, Jorja was simply stating facts.

He gave a wry laugh. 'No, I admit it doesn't sound much of a deal.' Ill at ease, he looked at her for what seemed to be a lifetime. She felt he wanted to say something, something important, something which would explain everything away, but of course there was no such facility. 'So,' he said eventually, 'where do we go from here?'

'How about eating cheese, finishing off the wine, and then calling it a day?' she suggested.

He laughed again, more easily this time. 'I do like a woman who knows when to take the initiative,' he said, robustly matching his mood to hers.

And I do like a man who knows when to give in gracefully, Jorja thought as they returned to the table. Mark had not given in gracefully, anything but.

CHAPTER FIVE

MELBOURNE is an attractive city. A visual treat of wide, tree-lined streets, beautiful squares and gracious buildings, it also has much to offer by way of friendly inhabitants, a wide range of cultural activities and an exciting nightlife. Jorja was happy to be there. The firm she worked for was constructing a shopping complex in Toorak, an élite suburb often simply called 'The Village', and she had been fitted on to the payroll as holiday relief. Since she had already spent three years in the States, her intention was to stay six months in Australia while she saw as much of the country as possible, then make her way leisurely home via Bali, Singapore and whichever parts of Europe her funds would allow.

Mark's arrival on the scene shortly before she was due to depart shattered her plans. A clever young architect, he had been asked to work as a freelance on the Toorak scheme. Already he had a stash of awards beneath his belt, though these gave him no airs and graces. Bejeaned, and with an unruly head of jet-black curls, he looked more like one of the beach bums who rode the surf than a hardworking professional who knew his craft inside out. Close-mouthed about his successes, he made a refreshing change from the pompous young architects Jorja had previously encountered. She warmed to him straight away.

And he had warmed to her. Within hours he professed to being bowled over, within days he announced he loved her, within less than a month he had proposed.

'Give me time!' she had protested, laughing and winding every wonderful word around her heart. He loved her! He wanted to marry her! She would be Mrs Mark Middleton.

'You can have all the time in the world, honeybun, though I insist on making love to you now. We are unofficially engaged,' Mark had pointed out when she looked doubtful. 'And the juice seems to go out of things if you wait too long.'

Swept off her feet, Jorja allowed her doubts to be swept under the carpet. Mark proved to be an urgent lover—too urgent at times. But these were the first heady weeks of a love which would last a lifetime, and she was content to wait for a deeper, steadier approach.

Although living together was common amongst the architect's circle of friends, he never once suggested they should follow suit. Jorja was surprised, yet also relieved. Their jump-the-gun lovemaking had demanded a major readjustment to her image of married life, and she had no wish to disrupt that image further. Maybe she was out of step in these days of casual pairings, but her dream of wedded bliss presumed a freshness, a sharing of newly discovered joys, and by living apart these were being deliciously hoarded for after the ceremony. A habit was formed. Two or three times a week she and Mark would dine out, maybe go dancing or to the theatre, then return to spend the night together at her bedsit.

'Your place is cosier than mine,' he always said, and she agreed. His place was a small pinched room overlooking the marshalling yards of a railway station.

'How can you live like this?' Jorja had asked, on the single occasion he had taken her there.

He had given a loose-limbed shrug. 'It's cheap, and I only touch down here occasionally anyhow.'

That a well-paid architect should choose such frugal accommodation had seemed odd, but Mark wasn't frugal in other ways—the ways which mattered. Every one of their nights at her bedsit spilled over with love. Yet as time passed another odd facet was revealed, his habit of disappearing without notice. Jorja accepted that he had a wide range of business commitments, but was hurt when he never took the trouble to tell her where he was going. Neither did he bother to telephone while he was away. And sometimes he disappeared for four or five days at a stretch. Jorja told herself she was fussing. Her mother fussed, and she must not be like her mother. To comfort herself she recalled how, in the early days of their meeting, Mark had expounded at length on how personal privacy was vital to him, and that life was infinitely more exciting when an element of mystery remained. She was not too sure how personal privacy and mystery existed within a marriage, but convinced herself—almost—that any lack of information as to his whereabouts must be an extension of this philosophy. Yet when Mark mentioned that he was to be away a fortnight, her queries tumbled out of their own volition.

'I'll be staying with an aunt in Canberra,' he said, admonishing her with a look. 'Any objections?'

'Er—none.'

'I'd ask you to come up for the weekend, but she's

not too keen on Poms.'

Poms? It was the first time he had used the wedge of nationality to separate them, and she grieved. But after the fortnight Mark returned to her side, and her bed, as though he had never left them.

Jorja's planned departure came and went, and not a word was said. At the office she had become the 'fix-it' girl, so nobody wanted her to leave. She meandered on. She and Mark had also begun to meander. Having agreed to give her all the time in the world, he now rarely mentioned the future. He was, she realised, one of those happy-go-lucky individuals who are content to confine themselves to the next twenty-four hours and let the rest go hang. He responded cheerfully whenever she slipped a reference to their marriage into the conversation, but somehow definite plans were never made. Mark was satisfied with the *status quo*. Stop fussing, she told herself. You know he loves you.

When Mark next announced a trip to Canberra, she wished him bon voyage and changed the subject. His absence seemed an ideal opportunity to reassess their relationship, yet all Jorja could focus on in the lonely evenings was how much she missed his smile, how she longed to feel his arms around her. And when a ring came on her bell early on the Sunday morning, she galloped down from her bedsit in a state of feverish delight. This had to be Mark. Vaguely he had mentioned returning next week, but missing her must have brought him back ahead of time. This separation had finally done the trick. He had grown impatient with the limitations of a love affair, and now needed an official liaison. There was a warm glow inside her when she opened the door.

'Are you Jorja Reynolds?' enquired the girl she found on the step. With a mousy-brown ponytail and scrubbed-clean face, at first glance her visitor looked like a schoolgirl. But a curly-headed little boy was clutching on to one hand, and a baby nestled in the crook of her arm. Early twenties seemed more realistic.

'I am,' she nodded.

To her astonishment, the girl's eyes filled with tears. Her lower lip trembled and she swayed. There was one frightening moment when she appeared on the point of collapse.

'I've come to ask if—if—' there was a sob, 'if you'll leave Mark alone. I need him. Ben needs him.' The girl cast down a look at the toddler, who gazed back with wondering brown saucers of eyes. 'Christabel needs him, too,' she gulped, when a tiny starfish hand waved from the bundle in her arms.

Jorja's mind spluttered and went *phut!* Blankly she stared at the trio; the girl, her eyes pink and puffy, the worried little boy, the baby who was immune to it all.

'I'm sure you can find yourself another man,' the girl continued. 'One who isn't already a husband and a father.'

'You mean——?' Jorja struggled to grasp the implications in three seconds flat, but failed. There had been a mistake, she decided, a dreadful mistake. Or perhaps this was a bad dream, and in a moment she would wake up?

'I'm Mae Middleton, Mark's wife.' The girl was hesitant and concerned. 'I'm sorry, I presumed you knew he was married.'

'No.' Jorja heard her voice come from afar. 'No, I didn't. I don't.'

How simple-minded could you be? The clues were there, had been there from the start. The absences, the living each day at a time, the airy-fairy frothy feel of love. Love? Her stomach cramped. Mark had a wife and children, what did love look like now? The beautiful garden of what they shared had been razed at a stroke. All that remained were weeds of squalid couplings.

'Could we go inside and talk?' her visitor suggested.

The stairs Jorja had galloped down moments ago now required to be scaled like Mount Everest. The little boy had begun to snivel. She wanted to snivel, too. Instead she went through the motions of making coffee for herself and Mae, then poured Ben a glass of orange juice.

'You didn't think anything was—odd?' Mae questioned. She had dried her tears and propped the baby up in the corner of the settee, and was now helping Ben with his drink.

Jorja shook her head. 'Mark never said much about his background, but I put that down to his being . . . casual. He did tell me he had an aunt in Canberra. I presume you live in Canberra?'

'No, East Richmond.'

Jorja groaned. East Richmond was less than five miles away, and now she realised that everything he had ever said to her could well be lies, lies, lies.

'Mark can be very plausible,' Mae said ruefully. 'He's created a cloud-cuckoo-land where he's a bachelor. He almost believes in it himself.'

'He does give the impression of being—unattached.'

'Mentally, he is.' Her visitor patted her arm. 'This must be a dreadful blow.'

Jorja smiled whimsically. 'We're doing this the wrong way round. I should be consoling you, and apologising. I do apologise. If I'd had the slightest inkling Mark was married, I would never——' Shame blocked her throat. 'Does he know you're here?' she asked, attempting a recovery.

'No. I told him I was taking the kids out to the park. I left him at home in bed.'

She felt queasy. Images of herself and Mark in bed kicked across her vision like bawdy chorus girls.

'He hasn't confessed?'

Mae grimaced. 'He never confesses. He believes if you don't talk about something, it doesn't exist.'

'Then——' Jorja gulped '—then this has happened before?'

'It has, though if it's any consolation you've lasted the longest. That's why I plucked up the courage to come and see you. His other women haven't meant much and the affairs soon petered out, but in your case——' Slender shoulders were shrugged.

His other women? Jorja felt lacerated. That was what she was, *the other woman!*

'How did you find out about me?' she enquired.

'A girlfriend of mine circulates round the edge of Mark's social circle. She keeps me informed.'

'By dropping hints?' Jorja asked, wondering if this so-called friend was the type of two-faced bitch who fed on gossip.

'She acts as an information service at my request,' Mae explained calmly. 'It only took a few months of marriage for me to realise that Mark and monogamy don't mix too well, and it seemed sensible to keep track of——'

'His other women?' Jorja cut in, lashing herself

with the phrase.

'Forewarned is forearmed,' Mae agreed.

'But if he's constantly unfaithful——'

'Why don't I leave him? Partly because the children need him, but mainly because I love him.' The girl paused. 'You must think I'm a doormat, letting him walk all over me like this, and I confess I'm not the most feminist of females, but there's no one else I'd rather live with. Even if he doesn't come home as often as he should.'

Jorja found this declaration unbearably sad. 'I won't see him again,' she promised, blinking back the tears.

'Thanks.'

Yet despite the haste with which she handed in her notice and booked her flight out of Melbourne, she did see Mark again. Two evenings later he came charging up to her bedsit, a bottle of champagne in one hand, flowers in the other.

'You bastard!' she said furiously, when he brushed cheerfully past her and into the room. 'Mae's been to see me. I know the truth, Mark. I know you're *married!*'

The word protruded like a bump in the road, but he skipped over it with what Jorja recognised as practised ease.

'I'm going to get a divorce.'

'Since when?'

'It's been on the cards for years.' He set the champagne and flowers aside, and reached out. Jorja kept her distance. 'Mae gave you a sob story and you fell for it?' he remonstrated. 'Let me guess, she arrived looking like a waif and stray, with the kids in tow? Jorj, Jorj, that was an act. The real Mae is as hard as nails. Her contribution to our marriage is minimal. Mae is cold and uncaring. That's why when I met you I couldn't resist you—you're warm, affectionate, sexy.'

'Sex! That says it all.'

'You're wrong. We go together well in so many other ways, you know we do. You support me, Mae never has. You inspire me, Mae doesn't.'

'Stop it!' If she had been a man, she would have punched him on the nose. 'You're a cheat and a liar! And a confidence trickster. How could you have the nerve to propose when you already have a wife? And what would you have done if I'd pressed to go straight ahead with our marriage—wriggled out or become a bigamist?'

'Honeybun,' he soothed, 'you're upset—Mae's upset you. But don't worry, when we're an old married couple we'll look back on this and laugh.'

Jorja kept a stony silence. The discovery that she had been carrying on an affair with a married man had brought her low, lower than she had ever been before. Once she had valued herself, now she felt cheap, soiled, tainted. How could she ever laugh about that?

'I'll fix an appointment to see a lawyer,' Mark continued, edging closer. 'Divorce is no great event these days. I don't know why you're making such a fuss. Just you wait and see, Mae'll fix herself up with a new daddy for the kids before the year's out!'

If any love had lingered, it ended then.

'What do you think marriage is, musical chairs?' Jorja demanded. 'You're Ben's and Christabel's father, and they need you. I don't intend to be the second Mrs Middleton, the wife who came after number one, but before number three. Get out! Get back to your family, that's where you belong!'

Mark went, only to reappear the next evening armed with chocolates and a well-honed line in you-mean-everything-and-Mae-means-nothing. The third evening she refused to open the door. The fourth she flew out of Melbourne's International Airport. The experience had been a harrowing milestone in her maturity.

When Jorja emerged from her room the next morning, she was tense. Dan might have given in gracefully, but after a night in which he had had a chance to realign his thoughts was he now ready to launch a fresh onslaught on her emotions? Terrified that he might sink to coaxing, wheedling, pleading, she eyed him warily as she joined him for breakfast. To her relief he greeted her cheerily, and made no mention of personal matters. Thus he gained her gratitude.

The day was busy. Incredibly, Lorenzo Cebrian arrived at the site office two minutes before nine, and they settled down to business. The hours until lunch were devoted to paperwork, then in the afternoon came discussions with the landscape gardener, and later a meeting with a representative from the local firm recruited to handle sales enquiries. As usual Dan alternated between being funny, electric and tough. Roaming round the cabin, he reminded her of a sensitised lion. No one was safe, yet no one wanted to be safe.

'Penny-pinching is crazy at this late stage,' he decreed, when the gardener complained of his creative impulses being stifled due to Lorenzo's

mercenary streak. 'First is first and second comes
nowhere. This development has the potential to be
the best on the island, so get to it!'

'*Sí, señor*,' grinned the gardener.

Next the organisation of the local sales office fell
beneath Dan's sights. Lines of communication
between Lanzarote and Chester had to be arranged,
plus advertising, rates of exchange, and a thousand
other matters. Jorja was deeply involved here, and
when the meeting ended she had a list of notes several
pages long. The local man, armed with his own list,
left mouthing promises to return the next day with
solutions to various problems which had been
identified.

They ate dinner at a nearby restaurant that
evening, rapidly returning to the apartment where
Dan spread cost sheets over the living-room table and
pondered, while Jorja scribbled initial sentences of
her purple prose. Then it was eight hours' sleep,
waking up to a sunny morning, another day at the site
office. And another.

'We've covered one hell of a lot of ground,' Dan
remarked, leaning back in his chair at the end of the
third day. 'The sales organisation is as far on as we
can get it, the gardener's knocking the grounds into
shape, and everything else appears to be on schedule.
Seems to me we've worked ourselves out of a job.' He
stretched contentedly, and grinned. 'What would you
say to some sightseeing tomorrow?'

She smiled at him across the desk. 'Yes, please!'

By mutual agreement, their destination was Timanfaya, Fire Mountain. As they drove into the heart of
the island the next morning, their route took them

through charming villages and fertile farmlands until—as if a line had been drawn on a ruler—came the contrast. The *malpais*, the badlands, began. Once again the landscape was lunar, but unlike the gravel plain these surroundings were dramatic. Razor-sharp and vicious, the lava which had been vomited out two centuries ago spread as far as the eye could see. And buried beneath the rock lay villages, gone for ever. The ferocity of nature was frightening. Awed by the darkly forbidding monotony, they both fell silent.

Dan and I are insignificant, Jorja thought, gazing into the distance where the majestic peak of Timanfaya shimmered through a heat haze. We're two specks, set on earth for a time which amounts to no more than a blink of an eye. What we do doesn't matter, not really. The sun will continue to rise and set, tides will ebb and flow, volcanoes will erupt, life will go on. Her introspection took on a more subjective slant. Hilary doesn't deserve to be considered, Toby's too young to know, so where's the harm if we combine? Nobody would be hurt, and . . .

'Would you like a ride on a camel?'

She looked at him and gave a startled laugh. Dan had rescued her. They couldn't combine. It was impossible, too dangerous, *wrong*.

'Lead me to it,' she said.

The Suzuki was parked halfway up the mountain, where they joined holiday-makers who were clambering aboard a line of long-suffering camels.

'Give me flying any day,' muttered Dan, clinging on as their steed levered itself upright in an ungainly wobble. They were seated in a basket arrangement, one on either side of the animal's hump, and their perch was precarious. 'Do you think these things are insured? The ground looks a very long way down.'

Swinging and swaying, they set off up the rocky slopes in single file. The caravan moved slowly, allowing a photographer to walk along and snap each pair of passengers in turn. 'Smile, please!' he yelled in three different languages, and Dan gritted his teeth in a cheesy grimace.

'The Bedouin won't find me hammering at the door of their recruiting office,' he groaned, staggering back to solid ground forty minutes later. 'As far as these ships of the desert are concerned, you can keep the lot!'

At that moment the photographer appeared beside them, brandishing a selection of hurriedly prepared prints.

'I'll have this one,' Jorja laughed, 'to pin up on my office wall.'

'You will not!' Dan retorted, peering over her shoulder at a photograph where she was perfectly at ease, while he was in the throes of some ill-concealed terror. 'It'd ruin my street credibility for ever.'

She was giggling as they climbed back into the four-wheel-drive. Forget introspection, forget about combining. Dan—as a friend—was good fun to be with.

Their next stop in the volcanic park was at the top of Islote de Hilario. Here they watched guides conduct a series of experiments to prove the fierce temperatures which burned just below the earth's surface. Hot cinders were scooped up and passed round, a bush tossed into a hole burst into instant flame, geysers were made to hiss skywards in plumes of scalding white steam.

Refreshed and rested after lunching on steaks grilled by the underground heat, they resumed their sightseeing. Past jagged cones and overhangs they travelled, in what they both agreed could be best described as nature's crematorium. Following the narrow road, they wound up peaks, then plummeted in tight, breathtaking bends down to tranquil valleys where the rock had been weathered to a fine grey grit.

Mid-afternoon they decided they had had enough of this moribund wilderness, and Dan pointed the Suzuki towards the coast. A swim was on their agenda, so Jorja studied the map. She navigated them to a beach on the southernmost tip of the island, known for the white smoothness of its sand. They were not disappointed. The sand was like flour and with rocks at either end, the tiny cove had a picture-book prettiness.

Jorja flung off the towelling shirt and shorts which covered her yellow bikini.

'See you later, slowcoach,' she grinned over her shoulder, as she headed down towards the sea.

She was on the point of stretching out a toe to test the temperature when from behind came the thud of feet and a suntanned male in black swim trunks streaked past, beating her into the water.

'Who's a slowcoach?' he demanded, splashing her.

Dan dived into the waves, arms moving in a powerful crawl. Naked, or nearly so because the trunks were brief, he had a disturbing effect. With regret Jorja was forced to admit that, although the atmosphere between them had been casual, since waking all of her had been centred on him; on the grey of his eyes, on the rich timbre of his voice, on the golden highlights the Lanzarote sun had already bleached into his hair. She waded deeper to dunk her head, and when he swam to her side was resolutely prosaic. Wasn't the sea clear? she commented. Did he know the name of the island in the distance? Had he noticed the wet-suited divers on a far rock? What could they be searching for?

'Who knows? Maybe sunken gold. The Canaries were thick with pirates and treasure ships in the eighteenth century. Nelson came here looking for booty and attacked the garrison in Tenerife. That's where his saluting arm was shot off. Not the most pleasant of holiday memories,' Dan added pungently.

They swam around for a while, and when they grew tired waded up through the powdery sand to stretch out on towels in the sun.

'Don't let my presence inhibit you if you feel the urge to strip off,' he teased, looking along the bay to where a group were sunbathing nude. He dropped a wicked eyelid. 'I'll just lie here on my stomach and show no reaction. Us Englishmen are like that, immune to life's ups and downs.'

He might be immune, she wasn't. Jorja lay back and closed her eyes, but the image of the bronzed body so close to hers burned like a brand on her brain. She sat up, hugged her arms round her knees and stared hard at the horizon.

'Shall we go for a walk?' she suggested.

Dan rolled over, propping himself up on his elbows. 'I'd rather not. I'm fine on solid ground, but my leg doesn't stand up too well in sand, and there's not much else available round here.'

Jorja cast a look at his damaged limb. Slightly withered, a network of silvery-white scars spread a surprising distance both above and below his knee.

'Was your leg badly broken?'

'There were several compound fractures. The

whole limb was badly mashed, so much so that at one stage the surgeon wondered about amputation.'

Her eyes widened in horror. Since she had been abroad then, she had never heard a full account of the crash and Dan's injuries.

'Things were that serious?'

' 'Fraid so. I also had internal bruising, abrasions to my body, plus a cracked rib or two.' Plaintively he began to play an invisible violin. 'I was in a very sorry state.'

'How long were you in hospital?' she asked.

'Just over a month.' His humour fell away. 'I was supposed to stay longer, but I ranted and raved and the surgeon agreed to discharge me ahead of time. Mind you, it was on the understanding that a physiotherapist came to the house each morning and took me through my paces.'

'Why the desperation to get home?'

'Well, my father had had his heart attack and——'

Jorja frowned. 'It happened so soon after the crash?'

'Three days after.'

'I never realised that.'

'The doctor reckoned his body broke under the shock of Jonathan's death. What the doctor didn't know was that another factor was involved, one which in my view——' Dan squinted against the dazzle of the sun on the ocean, and sighed. When he spoke again he neglected to complete the earlier sentence. 'Once my father was out of intensive care and back home, I felt I was wasting my time in hospital. I needed to be on hand to give him whatever comfort I could—which wasn't much. I felt so damned impotent.'

'It must have been a traumatic time.'

He nodded. 'Both of us were swallowing down daily doses of medication and not making much sense. We tried to do our best, but——' he sighed again, 'when that car went out of control, so many lives went out of control too. Jonathan's death has had far-reaching effects, though no one could ever have realised exactly how far-reaching they'd turn out to be,' he added sourly.

'You mean Suzanne?' questioned Jorja, not knowing what he was referring to.

'Suzanne? Oh, Jon's fiancée?'

'Yes. Pauline said something about her going to pieces after the crash. Didn't she rush off to the Himalayas and become the disciple of a guru?'

'I believe she did, but it didn't last long. She's been back in Chester for ages now. And she's reverted to type. She's married to a stockbroker, holds coffee mornings for charity, and wears sensible shoes. She's so damned dull it amazes me Jonathan ever managed to get himself worked up over her. He was rushing to meet Suzanne when we crashed,' Dan explained. He threw her a glance. 'Would you like to hear the whole grisly story?'

'If it's not too painful.'

'It's not. Not now.' He repositioned himself on his elbows and stared out at the sea. 'Jonathan and I had been invited to a party, but he'd quarrelled with Suzanne and because she was on the guest list he'd decided he wouldn't show. I was all set to go alone. Then she telephoned, and after some lengthy emotional caterwauling he changed his mind. By that time I had the car out of the garage and was on the point of departure, but he asked me to wait until he got ready.'

Dan shook his head in wry disbelief. 'When my brother got ready—wow!'

Jorja smiled. 'I thought it was only females who spend three hours in the bathroom?'

'If it is, nobody ever told Jonathan. For him it was the long shower, the shampoo, the shave, the aftershave, the fresh clothes, the hair-combing in front of the mirror. When he finally emerged I was frayed around the edges, to say the least. Then he announced we'd get to the party quicker if *he* drove! We had a barney, all about me being the kind of law-abiding fool who keeps within the speed limit, and about him driving with panache but no consideration. The outcome was that we hurtled off along the lanes with Jon at the wheel. To our amazement, a guy in a Porsche overtook us. Jon overtook on the next bend, but seconds later the Porsche got the better of us again. Jon's appetite was whetted, and a chase developed which had it been in a movie would have had the audience cheering.' Dan shuddered. 'In reality it was juvenile and dangerous.'

'Didn't you tell him to slow down?'

'Didn't I? God! I passed from "shouldn't you ease up a little?" to full-scale begging in minutes, but he took no notice. The hedgerows became a green blur, the bends loomed up like those in a Monte Carlo rally—zap, zap, zap. But all Jonathan could think about was the damn Porsche. When he attempted to overtake the next time, he cut it too fine. Another car was approaching, and to avoid a collision he was forced to swerve.' Dan's features hardened. 'He swerved into the side of a barn packed tight with bales of hay and the car crumpled like a tin can. When the ambulance reached us I was jammed up against the dashboard drifting in and out of consciousness, and Jon was dead.' He made a mindless pattern in the sand. 'Three days after that my father suffered his coronary, and a few weeks later I was married. Boy, was that a busy year,' he said bitterly. He brushed the sand from his hands. 'We'd better go. It's a fair distance back to the apartment, and Lorenzo's picking us up at seven.'

CHAPTER SIX

SEÑOR CEBRIAN'S disregard for punctuality meant that it was nearer eight when he arrived, and by this time Jorja had become the victim of a strange jumble of feelings. In preparing for the dinner date she had devoted considerable care and attention to her appearance. If Jonathan had been fussy, this evening she would have left him standing. There had been a shower, a shampoo, a careful blow-drying of her hair. Then she had frowned over her wardrobe for ages. She had tried on several outfits, and eventually picked out a raspberry silk top which was teamed with matching tapered trousers. The top had a boat-shaped neck and full sleeves, and murmured 'expensive boutique' with every thread. She knew she looked good in it.

Next her face had been considered. With her complexion lightly tanned there was no need for foundation, but she took time fingertipping dark gold shadow on to her lids, outlining her eyes with kohl, brushing her lashes with filamented mascara. Her lips were painted with a paler shade of raspberry. After applying the faintest touch of blusher, she smiled at her reflection in the mirror. Not only did she look good, she looked terrific. A pink chiffon bandeau was tied round her head in a pretty knot, French perfume sprayed on to pulse points, and she was ready.

On the balcony she found Dan, sipping wine and leaning on the rail.

'Hi!'

She did not pirouette before him, but there was an air of presenting herself for inspection—and admiration.

'Hi.' His eyes barely hit base. 'Sangria?'

'Please.' She watched as he moved to the rattan bar in the corner of the living-room to fix her drink. In an oatmeal-coloured suit and cream shirt, he was such a blond summer man that her heart twanged. 'You're looking very smart tonight,' she said, when he returned.

He lifted a laconic brow. 'What, in this old thing?' Jorja grinned. Surely now he would say how wonderful *she* looked? But again he barely seemed to notice her. 'I've been giving some thought to the advertising campaign,' he said, frowning out at the evening sky. 'I reckon that in addition to the national press, we should try one or two more localised papers back home.'

Jorja bristled. She felt like thumping him between the shoulder blades and saying to hell with business! Why couldn't he acknowledge that she looked stunning? He did not need to stagger back with arms raised on high and his mouth an oval of astonishment, but a faint interest, a slither of—yes, desire, on his part would have been flattering.

'Don't forget to keep up the pretence with Lorenzo that we've been occupying the two apartments,' he ordered, having crossed all the t's and dotted all the i's as far as the proposed advertising campaign was concerned. 'Before we leave tomorrow I'll make sure to muss up a bed in Number 230 and move things around to give the impression that it's been lived in. As far as this place goes, I've closed my bedroom door and removed all obvious signs of habitation, just as a precaution for when Lorenzo comes to collect us. *If* he ever comes to collect us,' he said, looking at his watch. Dan's brows came down. 'Whoever cleans this apartment's bound to realise both beds have been slept in so we must think up a reason for your having used both, just in case a query should crop up.'

Jorja gave him a plastic smile. 'Suppose we set fire to one, or marinate the mattress in rum and Coke, *Cuba Libre* for the uninformed?' she suggested, contrarily resisting his compulsion, obsession even, to provide the world with glaring evidence of an innocent relationship.

'If you consider this is a joke, then allow me to supply the punch line,' he rapped back. 'I happen to be in the process of divorcing myself from a woman who'll use any trick in the book to——' The doorbell shrilled. 'Lorenzo at last,' he said, and made for the hall. 'I can't imagine a reason for him to go into my room,' he flung over his shoulder, 'but if things look as if they're heading that way, change the subject quick.'

She slitted her eyes at him as he disappeared.

'Yes, sir.'

Dan was good fun to be with? Baloney! He spent the evening being flawlessly innocuous, flawlessly circumspect, flawlessly consistent as her businessman boss. Although Jorja accepted that he was being sensible, his attitude still made her seethe. Whatever vibes were around, Lorenzo picked them up and became so attentive that he and Jorja were rapidly welded into a jabbering duo, while Dan became the silent onlooker. The Spaniard's chatter was banal. At first Jorja kept glancing at Dan, expecting to detect amusement in the twitch of a brow, a crease at the corner of his mouth, but there was no reaction. She would have had more feedback from a stone sculpture!

She did not bother to ask herself why, but as the evening lengthened she grew into the flirty, flighty piece Señor Cebrian desired. She drank, she dallied, she dazzled. If her employer wished to treat her like a friend of a friend of a friend, that was up to him, but Lorenzo was treating her like a woman—a bewitching, seductive, beautiful woman. He appreciated her. She ignored the rolls of fat concertinaed around his waist, greeted every half-baked phrase he uttered as a literary masterpiece, and smiled, as starstruck as if he was the latest in male sex objects. His brother, hot from the kitchen, proved to be another middle-aged Romeo, yet Jorja laughed and fluttered her lashes in a way which, had she stood back and watched herself in action, would have made her want to curl up and die.

If, when they returned to the apartment, Dan had lambasted her for her performance, she would have meekly submitted to whatever he had chosen to fling, but all he said was, 'Goodnight.'

What had been good about it? she wondered, as she went into her room. She undressed, creamed her face, cleaned her teeth and climbed into bed. She lay on her back, conscious of the tall, blond man just a few feet away through the wall. She turned on to her side. To hell with him, to hell with Lorenzo, to hell with everything! Furiously Jorja wrapped the sheet round her, and began counting sheep. One, two, three, four, jumped over a fence. At twenty-five she heard a noise. The sheep froze mid-leap. Eyes wide in the dark, she waited. The noise came again, to be identified as measured cautious footsteps outside in the hall. Dan was on the move. Fervently she wished he would burst into her room and make mad, passionate love to her. Fervently she wished he would stay away. A tap on the door held her immobile, hardly daring to breathe. Then it registered that the tap had not been at *her* door. Puzzled, Jorja sat up. What was happening? She heard more soft footfalls, then silence. Was there an intruder? Maybe that thieving Pedro had materialised? Her eyes searched the darkness, looking for a heavy instrument with which to defend herself. But what about Dan? Was he to be attacked when he was sound asleep? She must warn him. Jorja was halfway across the room when she heard an exclamation, followed by a whirlwind of male voices, one fierce and demanding, the other apologetic. Next came a scurry of footsteps. She emerged from her room just in time to catch sight of a shadowy figure fleeing from the apartment as though the hounds of hell were in hot pursuit.

'Happy now?' enquired Dan, as the front door slammed shut. She jerked round to discover him a yard from her on the threshold of his room. He was naked. A shaft of moonlight silvered his hair and the width of his shoulders, but mercifully the rest of him was in shadow. 'Thanks to your behaviour earlier this evening, our fat Spanish friend decided to pay a visit.'

'That was Lorenzo?' she asked, her voice faint with surprise.

'Who did you think it was, the tooth fairy? And after the way you flung yourself at him I'm not the least bit surprised he had the hots for you. You didn't slip him a spare front door key while I was otherwise engaged paying the damn bill, did you?'

'No, I didn't. And I didn't fling myself at him

either.' Jorja was aware of firing a dud, but it seemed better than no retaliation.

'That's not what it looked like from my side of the table,' Dan retorted predictably, rubbing his chest and drawing her attention to the whorls of blond hair displayed there. 'What were you trying to prove?'

'Nothing.'

'No?'

'No!'

They stood and glared at each other through the darkness, then Jorja became aware of how his shoulders were beginning to quiver. He appeared to be in the grip of some intense emotion. She stood a little straighter, preparing herself for a second verbal attack. It was rare that Dan lost his temper, but when he did so he did it with gusto, radiating a readiness to take on all comers. Her heart tipped over. She was the only comer available. Fearfully she waited for the worst, but the emotion which gripped him proved not to be fury, but amusement. A chuckle started low down in his chest and bubbled its way to the surface. Another chased it. The chuckles grew stronger, until he ended up clutching at the door frame and rocking with laughter.

'I wish I'd had a film of that!' he gasped. 'If you could've seen Lorenzo's face when he pulled back the sheet and discovered me lying there instead of you—it was priceless. I don't know which of us was more surprised. Thank goodness he didn't decide to strip off in readiness for seducing me,' he added, and once again was laughing fit to bust.

Jorja remained straight-faced. Maybe Dan regarded what had happened as the most hilarious thing in ages, but the realisation that the Spaniard had actively pursued her was alarming. Suppose he had entered her room? Suppose she had lain alone in the apartment as Lorenzo had imagined, what then? Considering her earlier performance, she could scarcely blame him if he had refused to take no for an answer.

'Were you asleep?' she enquired starchily.

'Not quite.' Dan made an effort to control himself. 'I heard him knock, then I heard the bedroom door being opened. There were footsteps, and——'

'And what?' she prompted, when he halted.

His eyes met hers through the shadows. 'I thought it was you. I waited with bated breath, as they say.'

'Why—why would I come into your room in the middle of the night?' Jorja challenged tremulously.

'Because you find me irresistible?' It was not quite the joke he had intended it to be. His humour had separated from the spontaneity of a moment ago. Dan shrugged. 'However, the hand that peeled away the sheet was large and hairy, and the eyes which gazed down into mine were bloodshot. Lorenzo had been murmuring sweet nothings, but he stopped mid-flow. There was a moment when his brain refused to accept the message it was receiving from his eyes, then we both began gabbling—me accusing him of being a slimy old villain, which he is, and him offering profuse regrets.'

'And where does he think I am?'

'In the other apartment. Thank the Lord I had the presence of mind to tell him he'd got muddled up about which of us was where.'

'So now he's shot off up the hill looking for me?'

Her question winded him. 'I hope not! I fed him the information thinking that as he'd been caught he was bound to quit and go home to Señora Cebrian, tail between his legs.' Dan looked at her in dismay. 'Do you think he's likely to be on the rampage still?'

'No. You're right, he will have lost interest. And if he should let it drop that he paid Apartment 230 a visit, we can always say I heard of a cancellation, and decided to spend the night in a hotel.'

'For no apparent reason and without telling me? Doesn't ring exactly true, does it?'

'How else do you suggest we cover ourselves?' she demanded.

'Cover ourselves?' Dan grunted. 'Wonderful, isn't it? Other people have affairs like crazy, and never give a damn. Yet here's you and me concocting furtive little alibis to mask a grand romance which never happened.' He paused, and when he spoke again his eyes seemed to burn like lasers into her soul. 'I never realised it before, but there must be a strong streak of the masochist in me.'

The atmosphere began to crackle. Ever since he had rounded on her, Jorja had been overwhelmingly aware of his nakedness, but now his look told her she was scarcely more than naked herself. The all-in-one body skimmer she wore, the latest version of the teddy, was cut high on the thigh and low at the bodice. The cling of the oyster silk-satin revealed more of her figure than it hid.

'You think so?' she said chokily.

Dan's eyes dipped, moving across her breasts like stroking fingers. 'I know so.' Silence. Tension. He turned to rub his brow slowly back and forth against the jutting corner of the door frame, reminding her of an injured animal seeking solace. 'Why else would I have agreed to have you so near to me, and yet so far away?' His voice was low, a mellifluous throb in the stillness of the night. 'It's blatantly obvious how much I want you. I want to kiss you until our mouths are swollen. I want to make love to you so hard and so long that neither of us will be able to walk straight for a week.'

'Dan——' she murmured.

Moonlight paled his shoulders and the long sweep of his back, where the spinal furrow made a dark smudge. For weeks she had been telling herself she liked him, just liked, but could liking be responsible for this shortage of breath, the way every pore screamed to have him closer? Liking was a middle emotion, but what she felt now was no middle thing. It was turbulent, extreme. Here he was, this gorgeous, naked, aroused man, and . . .

'Go to bed, Jorja. Please!'

'Dan,' she said again, and without any help from her, her hand rose to caress his back. His skin was warm and smooth, like velvet. As she drew her fingers slowly down from his shoulder, she felt him tremble.

He turned. 'Sweetheart,' he said, in a strangled voice and drew her into his arms.

His kiss was an invasion, so fierce and greedy and relentless that her lips tingled. While one arm was wound round her waist, the other slid upwards until he entwined his fingers amongst the burnished hair at the back of her neck, pinioning her. He did not intend to allow her any escape, but Jorja did not want to escape. He kissed her again. And again. And again. As her head began to spin, his kisses became gentler, deeper. It was as if he was drinking honey from her. His mouth kissed its way across her cheek, and he pushed his face into her hair.

'Fragrant, like roses,' sighed Dan, breathing in. The fingers at the back of her neck relaxed, and he began moving his hand through the silken strands. 'You have beautiful hair—so rich, so curly, so full of life.'

Dimly she was aware of the pressure of his lips filling the hollow at the base of her throat. He sighed his delight, and began to nibble at the smooth curve of her shoulders.

'Mmm, sunburned skin. It tastes good. Jorja, I want to lick you. I want to lick every beautiful, beautiful inch.'

He eased the narrow straps from her shoulders and the silk-satin slid down, catching for an erotic moment on the peaks of her breasts before gathering softly round her waist. The touch of his fingers on her naked flesh was electric. Instinctively she arched, pressing the surging fullness of her breasts into his hands and murmuring as each nipple was moulded into rigid desire. Dan lowered his blond head, moistening the rose-brown tips with a fiery tongue, and she clung to him, hands on his waist, fingers splayed and grasping.

'Dan.' A low groan emerged from her throat. 'Oh, Dan. Darling Dan!'

Her endearment acted like a splash of cold water. He seemed to jolt. His head came up. 'No,' he said, and snatched his hands away. His retreat gathered momentum. 'No! No!' He rocketed back, eyes glittering like a wild man's. Chest heaving, he glared at her. 'What the hell are you playing at?' he demanded.

'M-me?' stuttered Jorja, unable to adapt to this whiplash change of mood.

'Yes, *you*. Have you forgotten how we're supposed to be steering clear of trouble?'

'But——'

'This is all your fault,' he accused, and with a step as correct as any Guards officer's he marched back into his room.

Jorja stared at the closed door in stunned amazement. She would have laughed—if she hadn't wanted to cry.

When Lorenzo Cebrian saw them off at the airport the next day, he was subdued. His mood was appropriate, for since they had joined forces at breakfast neither Jorja nor Dan had managed to string more than two sentences together. Both were uneasy. Both were involved in their own worlds.

Their recklessness the previous evening had been her fault, Jorja thought miserably, as Dan gave the Spaniard final reminders and commands. *She* had suggested they share the apartment. *She* had enticed Lorenzo. *She* had stroked Dan's back. And now, as he had previously asked, where did they go from here? Their relationship was beginning to have much in common with a roller-coaster ride. There were troughs of calm when they were workmates and friends, followed by a sudden breathless climb to a dizzy height when they came close to being lovers. Then down again—thud. But always there was the danger of the wagonette careering off the rails. Her head thrummed. How did they continue? They didn't, they couldn't not like this. But suppose Dan's divorce went smoothly, suppose he was free in a few months? A few months wasn't long, and if they restricted their meetings to the office . . .

'Farewell.' Lorenzo gave a chastened smile.

Their flight had been called and now was the time for goodbyes. They took their leave of the Spaniard, gathered up their bags, and walked out across the tarmac with the other passengers.

'Lorenzo didn't visit the other apartment,' Dan informed Jorja as they approached the plane. 'I did some discreet fishing, and it turned out he'd dashed straight for home.'

'Then we're safe?'

He looked straight ahead. 'It appears so,' he said drily.

'I presume you went over to Apartment 230 and dealt with the bed?' He nodded. 'Wouldn't it have been wiser to have gone in the car?'

His jaw tightened. 'What you mean is, "Oh look, Dan's limping again."'

'Well, you are,' she defended. At breakfast he had been fretting over his leg, but when she had made as if to comment he had thrown such a vicious glare that she had kept silent. Jorja could keep silent no longer. His leg had become a definite disability. Every now and again he was wincing. 'I'd say you walked too far.'

'Okay, I did,' he snarled, then sighed. When he spoke again, the anger had gone out of him. 'I didn't sleep too well last night, and when I was awake at dawn I decided to get up. I visited the other apartment, then continued walking. I was walking uphill and on uneven ground. Now I realise it was the wrong thing to do.' He gestured for her to go ahead of him up the plane steps. 'I'll be fine once I sit down and rest.'

Dan was not fine. All through the flight he was

shifting in his seat to stretch and bend his knee, and although he then assured her that everything would right itself once he could stand up and move around, it was not to be. When they landed in England and began the walk along endless stretches of corridor, he was in obvious pain.

'See what happens when you lumber yourself with sub-standard goods?' he said, making slow progress as he hobbled along. 'Everyone else gets to claim their baggage before you do.'

'I don't ask for perfection,' Jorja replied fluidly.

He shot her a glance. 'Don't you?'

By dint of pausing every few hundred yards they managed to reach the baggage carousel. Pale beneath his tan, and with a film of perspiration on his brow, Dan collapsed on to the nearest seat and made no protest when she went off to manhandle their suitcases. The luggage trolley did duty as a walking frame, enabling him to reach the car.

'Will you drive?' he appealed, and when she agreed he slumped beside her in silence. Little was said on the journey home. 'If you drop me off at the Old Vicarage and take the Merc back to your flat, you could pick me up on Monday morning,' he suggested, when they reached the outskirts of Chester.

'Before you decide about coming into work, I think you should see a doctor,' she protested.

'Hey, isn't it me who gives the orders around here?' he joked, but his grin was a shadow of its usual self. 'Tomorrow's Sunday. I'll feel better after a day's rest. I will,' he assured her. 'I'll also feel better after seeing Toby. Just you watch, he'll be waiting for me on the front porch, dancing up and down in his pyjamas. And when I get out of the car he'll damn near tear my trouser legs off demanding to be picked up. Or maybe not.' Dan pulled a wry face. 'Could be I'll get bypassed when he realises his beloved Jorja's in the car.'

It was dark when she swung the Mercedes on to the gravel drive of the Old Vicarage. With golden light streaming from the windows, the sturdy white house beckoned like a comforting beacon in the chill night. After the balmy temperatures of Lanzarote, now they were back in what felt like mid-winter.

'I wonder where Toby is?' frowned Dan, when no eager imp danced a reel of anticipation and pleasure on the doorstep.

'I expect he's in bed. It is almost nine o'clock.'

He nodded agreement, and as she went round to the boot began the slow business of painfully extracting himself from the car.

'Thanks for acting as stevedore,' he said, when she lifted his luggage on to the step. 'Thanks for everything.' He put his hand on her wrist. 'Jorja, on Monday you and I ought to sit down and talk. We——'

'Hello, Daniel, my love. Had a good trip?' enquired a mocking voice, and they both looked round.

Hilary had appeared in the doorway, the light from the hall outlining her silhouette. Her legs, in tight jeans and ending in high-heeled black boots, were set apart, and a black jacket over a white shirt gave her a fashionably raunchy look. With arms akimbo, her stance warned that here was a woman not to be trifled with.

Dan gave a muffled oath, his features growing grim. 'What are you doing here? I understood you were to be in France for another two weeks? Why

have you come back ahead of time?' He shot a
distraught look beyond her to the house. 'Where's
Toby?'

'Don't worry, I haven't kidnapped him.' Hilary
gave a sweet smile. 'He's fast asleep upstairs, has been
for ages. All that running around of his got on my
nerves so I packed him off to bed early. He wasn't
pleased. Come to think of it, neither was your father.'

'What do you want?'

His wife made innocent eyes. 'Must I want
something?'

'If you don't, it'll be the first time,' he replied, with
deadly implacability. 'Would you care to tell me what
it is?'

'If you insist. All along you've lived in terror of my
lousing up that so carefully prepared divorce of yours,
haven't you, Daniel? Just fancy, I *am* going to louse it
up.' Her fingers drummed a silent arpeggio on her
hips. 'I can't accept the terms as stated. I need
alterations.'

Listening on, Jorja began to slowly die. Dan had
spoken of spanners and here they were. Hilary was
tossing big, steel, destructive spanners, spanners
which could well chew up the divorce machinery and
bring it to a halt.

'Like what?' he demanded hoarsely. 'I've been
generous, too generous. God, I've fallen over backwards to——'

'For openers, your solicitor's attempting to finalise
things in what—July? August?' Hilary flicked a
golden length of hair from her shoulder. 'Hate to be a
nuisance, Daniel, but as far as that particular timing's
concerned you can kiss it goodbye.'

CHAPTER SEVEN

IT was the second Saturday in June, and it was raining. Jorja gazed out at the garden. The lawn made a slippery green rectangle, bushes dripped, even the yellow cabbage roses which framed the kitchen window looked sodden and forlorn. She lifted her eyes. In the meadow cows were huddled together, trying to find shelter beneath the branches of a spreading oak.

'Rotten weather, isn't it?' commiserated Anne, when she sighed. Her stepmother was standing at the pine table, working lard into flour with cheerful abandon rather than expertise. 'And guess which bright spark's chosen to spend the afternoon tramping round a golf course and getting soaked to the skin?'

'My ever-lovin' father. He must be crazy!'

They both laughed, but as she returned to the view Jorja's amusement stilled. Her sigh had been misinterpreted. The wet June afternoon did not bother her, a cold March evening did. For almost three months the image of Hilary spouting her weasel words had haunted like a malevolent ghost which had taken up residence inside her head, and to her irritation she found herself reliving the scene yet again.

The blonde had been so smug, so gleeful, so damned certain she was the one calling the shots—which, of course, she had been. Jorja fingered the fine gold chain round her neck. At his wife's announcement Dan had muttered, then, with fists clenched, had bellowed, giving vent to his frustration in a mouthful of curses—curses which had made Hilary laugh. Hands on hips, head thrown back, she had laughed and laughed, delighted because the joke was on him. Jorja for her part had stumbled through a goodbye, reeled into the car and driven away. How she had reached the flat without damage to herself, the Mercedes, and/or any people who had been out on the streets that night, had been a miracle. Once there, she had sped past an astonished Pauline and locked herself in her room. The tears had come, to be followed by hour upon hour of anguished mental to-ing and fro-ing. In the silent hours of the night, she had accepted the grim inevitability. She must leave. Leave Lecomber & Co. Leave Chester. Leave Dan. Jorja recognised that she must go—now. One more day in his company, another sight of his lopsided smile, and it would be too late.

Hilary's laughter had been as effective as a pillow, smothering the newly born temptation to continue working with Dan until he was free. A few months of biding their time, allowing their relationship to develop as they waited for his divorce to come through would have been possible. Not easy, but possible. As long as there had been hope of a future, Jorja would have been prepared to stay put. But there wasn't a future, not a foreseeable one, and staying put could only lead to an involvement which contained more explosive devices than a minefield. That sexual buzz was the danger. It could not, would not, be held in check. And all that would be needed was one unguarded smile, a reckless hug to be noticed—maybe by busybody Elsie?—and the rumours would

fly. Rumours which would destroy Dan's reputation
as a solid citizen, and thrust her once again into the
despised role of 'other woman'. And suppose those
rumours reached Hilary's ears? The blonde might
well react maliciously. Having already demanded
alterations, might she not go further and withdraw
her consent for a divorce, simply to spite them? Or
block Dan in his seeking custody of Toby? Or use the
situation to drain her husband of his every last penny?
Or, or, or—the scenarios were endless. Hanging on
grimly could not be contemplated. For Dan's sake, for
Toby's sake, for her own sake, she must make a hasty
exit.

'I trust you realise I don't make apple pies for just
anyone?' said Anne behind her. 'Or at the drop of a
hat. Frozen food and carry-outs are more my style.'

Jorja nodded towards the bowl of gluey-looking
dough. 'So that's a special goodbye gift?'

'Very special, though I'm sorry it's required. You
could've stayed longer, you know. Your dad and I
have enjoyed having you here.' Her stepmother
kneaded the dough into a ball. 'Still, our loss is the
Palisade's gain, and if this turns out to have a
crippling effect on your digestion at least you're
guaranteed Cordon Bleu canteen lunches from Monday on.' Rolling out the pastry, Anne sneaked her a
glance. 'I realise public relations lady at a glossy
London hotel is an up-market job, but wouldn't
heading back north to Chester be . . . better?'

'I can't go back.'

'Can't?' Anne pushed aside a fringe of greying fair
hair, leaving floury streaks on her brow in memoriam.
'You don't mean ever?'.

'Not yet,' Jorja adjusted.

What was there to go back for when Dan had not been in touch? she wondered, twisting the golden chain round her finger. Although she had fled without leaving .a forwarding address—indeed, she had threatened Pauline with being hanged, drawn and quartered if she dared reveal her destination—he could have made contact. Wasn't her father's home the obvious place in which to seek her out? Sometimes she wondered if she had headed here because it was obvious, but whatever her motives, they were inconsequential. There had not been so much as a phone call, and she knew what that meant. Hilary continued to call the shots. At best Dan's divorce must be stationary, at worst sliding backwards.

'Shall I prepare the apples?' offered Jorja.

'Please, pet.' The pastry had been divided. Half was spread over the pie dish, while the remainder waited to form the top crust. 'Believe me, I'm not advocating that marriage should be treated lightly,' Anne began, crossing to the sink to wash her hands, 'but it is a high-risk business. From what you've told me this Dan of yours sounds to be a most honourable guy, so wouldn't it——?'

'He's not my Dan. We were attracted to each other but it was just a beginning.'

It was *just* a beginning, Jorja insisted to herself, slicing through the green-white flesh of a cooking apple. No matter how turbulent her emotions had been that night in Lanzarote when she had been unable to keep her hands off him, nothing had been established. Dan had never said he loved her, and she had never said she loved him—because she didn't. Admittedly it had been a near thing, but now it was over and she was doing her best to work him out of her system. So far she had not been having much success, but she was sure that once she reached London she would feel more resilient, once she had a challenging new job to occupy her mind, once she met new people.

'Then why are you finding it so difficult to pick up the pieces?' enquired Anne, showing an annoying determination to stick to her subject.

'I'm not!'

'No? Ever since you arrived you've been mooching around like one of the walking wounded. As I was saying, your Dan appears to be attempting to deal with a tricky situation in the best way he can. Don't you think——'

'There was no commitment on either side.' Jorja felt hot and cross. 'We hadn't become properly involved. We hadn't!'

'Pet, I understand how the prospect of being tangled up in a divorce can make your skin crawl. It did mine but——'

'The drowned rat has returned,' she cut in, hearing a peal of chimes from the front door. 'Hadn't you better go and greet him?'

Saved by the bell! she thought, as her stepmother hurried out. When she had first arrived in the Cotswolds, she had been desperate to talk. Anne had seemed the ideal recipient for her confidences, and it was true she had been both sensitive and understanding, but Jorja had rapidly discovered drawbacks to her candour. For some reason the older woman had taken a liking to Dan, whom she had never met, and begun rooting for him. Consequently, attempting to relegate him to a 'has-been' had been like fighting against a headwind. She tossed the cores and apple peelings into the pedal bin. Her stepmother was a romantic, and because her own love story had had a happy ending she stubbornly believed a pretty pink paradise lay in store for everyone else. Jorja was more realistic. With Dan out of reach, the only option she had was to shift her horizons and line them up with what was possible. Where was the sense in going into a downward spiral over what might have been?

She had been staring into space, but now she noticed a lack of whoops of delight and noisy kisses from the hall. In addition to being a romantic, her stepmother was an exuberant animal. When she greeted her husband, she did it in style. Unlike the first Mrs Reynolds, who had a habit of looking everyone, family included, up and down before backing off with an expression which made you wonder if she had recently been peeling lemons with her teeth. Jorja had no wish to be disloyal, but it had to be admitted her mother's demeanour was that of frigid greyhound, whereas Anne was the eager spaniel. She cocked her head, but all she could hear was the polite murmur of voices. Had someone called collecting for charity? Perhaps the milkman needed to be paid? She had begun arranging the fruit on the pastry base when her stepmother called.

'There's someone here to see you, pet.' She heard the delight in Anne's voice. 'He's driven down especially from Chester.'

Grief, it was Dan! Jorja froze, she shook, she died a thousand deaths. After three wretched months, he was here. He was standing only a few yards away in the hall. Her horizons underwent a dramatic revamp. Had he come hotfoot with the news that Hilary was finally co-operating? Please. Please. Please. Her heart pounded unevenly behind her breastbone, then her spirits sank. Wasn't it more likely that Dan had lost patience with waiting for a divorce and was here to plead the case for their joining in a discreet alliance, a secretive alliance, a furtive alliance? No, no, not that. Her sense of rightness, of morality, of self-esteem, must insist that she refused. Whatever it was she felt for him, she could never be his mistress.

Arms flailing like a demented octopus, Jorja wiped her hands, thrashed order into her hair, tugged at the neck of the white top she wore with an azure-blue jump suit. Gripping her hands on the wide, white leather belt which clinched her waist, she marched out into the hall. But the man who had driven down from Chester was Thomas Lecomber. Seeing him, she felt a stomach-twisting plunge of disappointment.

'What's the matter?' she demanded, as panic rapidly trundled disappointment aside. 'Why are you here? Is it Dan? Has he had an accident?'

Her visitor shook his silver head. 'Dan's fine. Actually, he was all set to drive down himself, but there was a phone call at the last minute. He had to go to some urgent meeting or other. I've come in his place. It's—it's about Toby.'

'Toby?' she echoed, her panic returning.

'He's all right,' came the swift reassurance. 'At least, there's nothing seriously wrong. But he had a severe dose of measles a few weeks ago, and his recovery isn't as rapid as it should be. The doctor can't explain why, but Toby's listless. He misses you, Jorja. He talks about you every day. He'd love to see you again, so Dan and I thought maybe——'

'Shall I make some tea?' Anne interrupted. 'If you'd like to go into the lounge I'll bring it through in a minute or two.'

'Thanks.' Jorja gave a grateful smile, then helped her visitor off with his raincoat and led the way. Comfortably cluttered with yesterday's newspapers, and dotted with bright zig-zag rugs and hand-thrown pots which spilled with flowers, the room contrasted with the sombre, pin-neat surroundings over which her mother presided. 'Tell me about Toby,' she begged, when Mr Lecomber was settled in a wing-back chair.

'He's a dejected wee soul. Antibiotics have cleared up the spots and nasty cough, but he's still not our Toby. He needs a boost, a tonic. That's why I'm here.'

'How did you know where to find me?' Jorja suddenly thought to ask.

'How did I find the village? Why, your stepmother gave Dan directions. Very clear ones, too.'

She frowned. 'They've been in touch?'

'We have,' Anne confirmed, breezing in with the tray. 'I have a confession to make. Dan phoned the day after you arrived, and since then I've supplied a few reports on your progress.'

'My—my progress? You've been—been talking to him on a regular basis?' Jorja spluttered indignantly. 'And you never said a word? I think that's——'

'No bad language, pet.' Her stepmother lifted the teapot. 'He needed to know you were safe.'

'You could have told me he'd rung!'

'If you're agreeable, maybe I could take you back to Chester with me now?' Mr Lecomber cut in. 'You could spend the night at the Old Vicarage and return tomorrow? Or you're welcome to stay longer if you wish?' he added hopefully.

'Thanks, but I'm afraid that's impossible,' Jorja

replied, having no alternative but to leave her resentment at Anne's duplicity simmering while she dealt with this suggestion. 'I've been working locally as a temp, but on Monday I'm joining the public relations team at a new hotel which has opened near Hyde Park.'

'Then you'd be able to come, so long as I have you back here in decent time tomorrow?' Mr Lecomber insisted.

'I suppose so.'

'There's only me, Dan and Toby at home—and the housekeeper, of course. We haven't seen Hilary for ages,' he emphasised, as though her reluctance might stem from a fear of coming face to face with Dan's wife. 'She did call in once to collect some clothes, but that was weeks ago.'

Once again the gold neck chain was being wound round her finger. Hilary would not be a problem and neither would time, because she did not have to present herself at the Palisade until Monday noon. Even so, Jorja hesitated. She felt torn. On the one hand she longed to see Toby again, and yet over the past months she had been painstakingly assembling a carapace, an emotional shield of sorts. The carapace was required for self-preservation purposes. Without it she suspected that she might well become maudlin about Dan. Yet it remained horribly fragile. If she set eyes on him again, would it shatter?

'Would you like milk or lemon, Mr Lecomber?' enquired Anne. 'Sugar, or can I get you sweeteners? And how about a biscuit?'

Poor Toby, Jorja thought, as the old man was provided with all he needed. With so many emotional bullets bursting around his little head, there was no way he could escape being caught up in the crossfire one way or another. Perhaps one way was this listlessness? At three years old he would not understand his mother's waywardness, his father's tension, her own sudden departure, but he had to be a victim. Her throat stiffened. She must provide whatever help she could.

'I'll be packed in five minutes,' she told her visitor, as he took an almond finger. 'But I won't accept your offer of accommodation. I'll stay with Pauline. She'll be offended if I don't.'

Incessant rain made the three-hour drive treacherous. Some minor roads were flooded, and when they reached the motorway mist sprayed up by other vehicles proved to be a constant hazard. Visibility was poor, and the windscreen wipers needed to work full-time. With Mr Lecomber devoting himself to the safe handling of his Rover, conversation was kept to a minimum. For this Jorja was thankful. Any conversation would be bound to contain a reference to his son, which sooner or later meant his marriage and divorce, but an awareness of the old man's unease meant that she balked at such subjects being raised. Also she had no idea what he knew about her and Dan's relationship, or why she had packed in her job overnight, so all round it seemed the less said the better. One thing was certain: her rash hopes about Hilary co-operating had been way off mark. Mr Lecomber would never have been able to keep such wonderful news to himself.

Saying less rather than more was becoming a habit, she thought wryly. Her mother, Pauline and Bruce had all received letters quoting garbled phrases about

the wanderlust striking again, and how she had taken
a sudden fancy to a change of scene on the work front,
but subsequent replies had indicated that not one of
them believed her, and all of them were confused.
Jorja gazed out at the misted length of motorway
which stretched ahead. The only person to whom
she'd said more rather than less was Anne, and look
what had happened there! Her stepmother had been
talking about her behind her back—for months. How
could she stoop to such a thing? More important,
what had she said? It was Dan's fault, he should never
have got in touch, she decided in a fit of pique. A
complete break must be best. But at least now she
understood why Anne had been championing his
cause. Who could resist that polished gravel voice?
Who could resist Dan? Jorja watched the lash of the
windscreen wipers and prayed that she could. Her
heart might have insisted she should make the
journey, but her head was warning of dire
consequences.

'You pop under cover while I put the car in the
garage,' Mr Lecomber instructed when he drew to a
halt outside the Old Vicarage. 'I'll bring your bags.'

Head down in the rain, Jorja scuttled out. The front
step was empty, but somewhere between her leaving
the Rover and arriving on the porch the door must
have opened, because when Jorja stood up straight
she found herself slapbang against Dan, a beaming
Toby in his arms.

'Oh!' she gasped. She gave a weak smile, a nervous
laugh, and began a desperate hunt for words with
which to compose a suitable greeting.

Fortunately Toby came to the rescue. 'Jorja!' he
cried, launching himself from Dan to her like a

wriggling rocket. His arms came round her neck in his throttling hold, kisses were peppered all over her face, and then he burrowed his head into her shoulder like a little rabbit burrowing into a hole. 'My Jorja,' he sighed.

Dan watched on. 'Hello,' he said softly. 'Thanks for coming.'

'That's okay. I——' A bone seemed to have stuck in her throat. Further words refused to come. All she could do was cuddle Toby close while she looked at Dan. While she looked at that lean, tanned face. While she looked at the thick blond hair which fell across his brow. While she looked into those grave grey eyes—eyes which said he had missed her as much as she had missed him. Eyes which said he *cared*.

Toby pulled back. 'You're crying,' he accused. 'Your face is wet.'

'Jorja's happy to see you,' Dan told him, when she remained mute—sniffing and blinking, and feeling stupid. 'Sometimes people cry when they're happy.'

The little boy gave him a most suspicious look. 'Would you like to see my spots, Jorja?' he enquired conversationally.

She smeared a hand across her cheeks. 'I—I thought they'd all gone.'

'They have,' confirmed Dan.

'Not all of them.' Toby yanked his T-shirt from the anchorage of his trousers and frowned down at a flawless tummy. 'There's one,' he insisted, jabbing himself with a finger.

'Never.' Mr Lecomber had joined them. 'Come along, let's go inside. It's nearly dinner-time, and I'm sure Jorja must be longing for a sherry. I most certainly am!'

The crisis was over. Her tears dried, and Toby allowed no opportunity for their return because in the hours which followed he was constantly demanding her attention. Chattering away non-stop, he brought toys to show her, insisted she play games, climbed on to her knee every five minutes. After dinner he announced that she, not Dan, must give him his bath, then she was instructed to read a bedtime story. His final demand, once his grandfather had been kissed, was that both she and Dan should take him upstairs.

' 'Night-'night,' Jorja smiled, tucking the little boy into bed.

He held out his arms. ''Nother cuddle. You feel nice,' he murmured, when she bent to him. Toby spread his hand on her chest. 'All soft.'

Dan stepped forward. 'It's very late. You've had a lovely time creating mayhem, but now I don't want to hear another peep out of you until morning.'

Toby grinned over the covers. 'Say squidgebonks,' he requested.

'Squidgebonks. Straight to sleep,' ordered Dan through the giggles.

'Yes, Daddy.'

'I mean it,' he rumbled, mock-Victorian papa for a moment before he kissed the three-year-old.

'Sleep tight,' said Jorja, as they retreated from the bedside.

'Mind the bugs don't bite,' recited a little voice.

There was another giggle, then silence. Dan switched off the light and closed the door.

'Have you ever noticed how that kid's obsessed with wanting to touch your breasts?' he muttered, as they walked along the landing. 'Which makes two of us. Jorja, I——'

She shied away from the arm which seemed to be preparing to enfold her. 'Your father said Toby was listless, but he seems his usual energetic self.'

'He's a quick-change artist. I know it's hard to believe on today's showing, but he has been down, very down. When the measles were at their worst he lay in bed with the curtains drawn and hardly said a word for days. And since then he's been apathetic.'

'Why wasn't he vaccinated?' Jorja asked hurriedly, fearful the man beside her might change tack and return to talking about her breasts, and his obsession with them. 'Isn't that the normal thing these days?'

'I believe so, but I left inoculations and such to Hilary. Because I knew she'd taken him along for jabs when he was a baby I presumed everything which was needed had been done.' Dan halted at the head of the stairs. 'It turned out there'd been omissions.'

'But you've had them attended to?'

He smiled, appreciating her concern. 'Don't worry, the doctor's made sure Toby's up to date on everything.' He spread a hand over the globe which topped the banister post. 'Touch wood, he shouldn't be brought so low again.'

Her eyes went to his hand. He had a big-boned, competent hand, slightly tanned and with a smattering of golden hairs across the back. Gazing at it, Jorja remembered his touch. Excitement tremored through her. She very much wanted him to touch her again.

'Then he'll have been protected against polio and smallpox and—and whooping cough?' she rattled. A lifeline was needed if she was to be dragged from this sudden quicksand of desire, and the only lifeline she could think of was speech. 'Oh, and diptheria. What else?'

Dan raised a brow. 'You want me to produce a list?'

'Well—no.' Flustered, Jorja searched her mind for some other topic of conversation. 'Do you think my coming here today has helped any?'

'I'm sure of it. Toby's been reassured. Now he knows you do still exist.'

'My . . . bowing out was troubling him?' she asked tentatively.

'It hit him hard which, when you consider the fickle way his mother's come and gone throughout his short life, isn't surprising. He'd imagined you were permanent. It turned out you weren't.'

Dan was using a matter-of-fact tone, but even so his words sounded like a condemnation. Jorja felt dreadful.

'Why did you say I'd gone?'

'I concocted a story about your father having been taken ill and needing to be nursed, but I suspect Toby never quite believed me. I don't think many people did, including Elsie.' He moved his hand, rubbing the wooden globe with a circular motion of his open palm. 'But some kind of explanation was required. Naturally I told my father the truth, a censored version.'

'The truth?' she enquired, interested to hear if his truth coincided with hers.

'That you weren't prepared to make up any kind of triangle.'

The description was apt, yet hadn't there been a tinge of criticism?

'You don't blame me, do you?'

'No, but——' Dan glanced at her from beneath his

lashes. 'Tonight, when my father's out of the way, you and I are going to have a long discussion.' An urgency was gathering. 'And I do mean long, so don't expect to escape upstairs early.'

'I'm not staying here.'

'You're not?'

'No. I'm going over to Pauline's. I did tell your father,' she defended, seeing his irritation.

'Cancel it. Hell, Pauline won't mind, and it's important we——'

'I can't.' I can't spend the night in this house with you, Jorja thought. I daren't. Last time it was my fingers that did the walking, along your spine. But now there's a danger my legs might walk, along the landing, into your room, into your bed. You're not a has-been. You never were, and I'm heartbreakingly afraid you never will be. 'The girl who followed me into the flat left a fortnight ago,' she continued steadily, 'and Pauline isn't keen about staying there on her own. A few days back she wrote asking if I'd come and have a weekend with her, and——' This excuse was supposed to sound calmly adult and truthful, but she had a nasty suspicion it was coming over as gibberish, lying gibberish at that. Her friend was sturdily self-reliant. Sleeping alone in the flat did not bother her one jot. 'And—and I feel it's my duty to see her,' Jorja finished lamely.

Dan gave her an impatient glance. 'When would you like me to run you over?'

Now, she wanted to say. Instead she shrugged and smiled. 'To suit you.'

Murmuring something about ten o'clock, he led the way downstairs to rejoin his father.

'How's your leg?' enquired Jorja, as he dumped

himself down beside her on the chintz chesterfield.

'Fine. The trouble cleared up after a couple of days. I'd just been overdoing things.'

'You should take more care,' Mr Lecomber chided from the depths of an armchair. 'Accept your limitations.'

He pressed his lips together. 'Yes, Dad.'

With Toby no longer dancing around, the atmosphere had changed. Having been annoyed to hear she was not staying the night, Dan now found his father's presence irksome. His frustration at not being able to talk to her alone, and at length, was obvious. The words he had bottled up inside were stampeding to be let free. Jorja pulled at a glossy brown curl. But she did not want to hear them. Those words must remain stoppered. Her reason in coming here was to see his son, not to allow Dan to breathe new life into an illicit relationship.

'How are things at the the office?' she enquired, needing to fill the silence.

'Okay. Sally, my new P.A., isn't up to your standard, but she's adequate. Our Brucie seems to like her,' Dan said drily.

'That's nice. Er—have you had any offers for Mellor Lodge?'

'Not one. Everybody takes a look at that ballroom of a hall, visualises the heating bills, and vroom!' His hand made an off-the-blocks rush. 'They can't get away fast enough.'

'Who can blame them?' piped up his father. 'It's my considered opinion there's no better value for money than a bungalow. I'd like a bungalow myself. There are too many stairs here,' he told Jorja. 'When you get to my age you prefer to have everything on one level.'

Dan lay back and spread his long legs. 'Here we go again!' he sighed.

'I mean it, Daniel. Just you wait and see, one of these days I shall move into a bungalow.'

'It'd be like moving into a shoebox. After spending years here being able to stretch, you'd hate it.'

'I'd love it. Remember the place I dragged you along to see out Sandbach way? You must agree that was——'

Toby did not possess a monopoly on chatter. Now Mr Lecomber regaled them with descriptions of bungalows past, present and, he insisted, future. When Dan looked at his watch and explained he must ferry Jorja over to her friend's flat, the old man insisted on their all having a nightcap. More stories of bungalows followed, and by the time they managed to escape and head out to the Mercedes, it was approaching eleven.

Dan barely gave her time to sit beside him and close the door, before he wrapped his arms round her.

'Sweetheart,' he sighed, and reached over to kiss her.

'I don't think——' Jorja began, but his mouth came down, obliterating her protest, obliterating her thoughts, obliterating everything. Somehow his kiss contrived to be fierce yet gentle, soft yet aggressive. Mouth against mouth, Jorja felt that heady magic.

'When you cried, you damn near had me crying, too,' he said, his voice barely more than a whisper, and the lips against her cheek moved into a smile. He stroked her hair. 'I know this isn't the ideal time or place for serious discussions, but even so——'

Jorja withdrew. 'Has Toby lost weight?' she asked.

'What?' Dan had been left behind.

'When he was in the bath I thought he'd dropped a few pounds. How many?'

The elder member of the family had had his say that day, likewise the junior one, but the middle Lecomber must be gagged. Serious discussions could only be about their getting together, maybe about their living together, and she must say no, no, *no*!

He sighed. 'I haven't a clue.'

'Doesn't it make sense to stand him on the scales from time to time?'

He switched on the ignition with a decided air of irritation, and the Mercedes sprang to life. 'I suppose so.'

'You could keep a record.'

'I could. Look, Jorja——'

'Mind you, even if he has lost weight I'm sure he's taller. Perhaps he's just lost baby fat and from now on he'll be skinny.' She looked at him as he swung the car out on to the road. 'Like his father.'

'His father wasn't skinny,' muttered Dan, moving up a gear.

'You were! Admittedly I wasn't around when you were three, but as a schoolboy——'

'You're missing the point,' he said heavily. He pressed his foot down on the accelerator, and the car gathered speed. 'Toby isn't my son, he's Jonathan's.'

CHAPTER EIGHT

'JONATHAN'S?' she repeated in astonishment.

'It's a closely guarded secret, and legally Toby *is* mine. My name appears on his birth certificate as his father, and there's no way to prove otherwise. Ninety-nine per cent of the time I've no desire to prove otherwise.' Dan slid the car into fifth. 'But I reckon I've already delayed too long in setting the record straight with you.'

Jorja stared at his profile. She had never heard the slightest whisper of doubt about Toby's paternity, had always assumed it was as it appeared, and now found herself struggling to absorb the disclosure and all its ramifications. 'Is your father aware of this?' she enquired, after a minute or two of hard thinking.

'He is.'

'He knew you—you weren't responsible from the very—from when Hilary first became pregnant?' she faltered.

'He's always known the truth. Why?'

She frowned. 'Because he once told me your marriage was at his insistence, but——' Her voice rose a step. 'But if that's the case it means he must have pushed you into marrying Hilary knowing full well the child she carried wasn't yours.'

Dan's eyes were fixed on the road. 'Who says he pushed me?' he demanded, and the harsh tone warned she had touched a nerve.

'Didn't he?'

His grip tightened on the steering wheel. 'My father persuaded.'

'Was there much difference?'

They were approaching a road junction. When the red light shone he braked, slowing to a halt. 'Okay, you win,' he sighed, meeting her gaze. 'I guess I'm only pretending I made the decision myself because admitting I was steamrollered does nothing for my ego. Yes, my father did push me, though a wide spectrum of reasons were involved,' he added, in a belated rearguard action. He waited until the lights turned from red to yellow and yellow to green, then drove on. 'If I'm to explain about Toby, I need to start with Jonathan,' he said, when they were cruising along the avenues towards the city centre. 'You'll remember his reputation as a stallion? What he experienced at sixteen took me until I was twenty-two to muster,' he remarked cryptically. 'Throughout our adolescence, if the phone rang you could guarantee it'd be some female desperate to speak to him. I always felt like Don Juan's retainer when we went out together. Women came at him full pelt from all angles, while I was ignored.'

'Perhaps you never gave out the right vibrations?' she suggested.

'Perhaps.' He pulled a face. 'One thing's for certain, my brother's vibrations were magnetic. They attracted females young, middle-aged, old. White, black, polka-dot.'

'Some must have resisted,' remarked Jorja, with a sideways glance.

'I never noticed them.' Dan was dismissive. 'When

Jon was in his teens the manner in which he played the field meant irate parents became an occupational hazard. He was repeatedly leading someone's darling daughter astray. My father went through torment.'

'Did he?' She gave a surprised laugh. 'I always had the impression he accepted Jonathan's escapades. You know, a boys-will-be-boys kind of attitude.'

'That was the front he adopted in public, but privately he found Jonathan's behaviour deeply embarrassing, and painful. Dad told me once he felt somehow he'd failed him, that if my mother had still been alive Jonathan would never have been such a tearaway.' Dan turned the Mercedes on to the first of the shopping streets. Here spotlit displays of smart fashions for the county set filled department store windows. Coats, trousers and shoes in ruby and sapphire shades indicated the season's vogue of jewel colours. 'My father used to issue warnings, lecture for hours, vow he'd cut him off without a farthing if he didn't mend his ways, and for a while Jon'd tread on tiptoe. Then a pretty girl would catch his eye and off he'd go again.'

'Hooked on women,' she said pithily.

'They were like a drug' he agreed. He peered ahead. 'Do I take the next on the left?'

'No, the one after.'

'When Jonathan reached twenty-one there wasn't much my father could do except appeal to his better nature, but he was wasting his time. Jonathan didn't possess a better nature, he was purely and simply amoral.' Dan paused as they left the brightly lit main street for a shadier cobbled lane. 'And great fun. You knew he was acting selfishly, insincerely, and you disapproved, yet when he lauged and said, 'Let's go', you found yourself rushing to join him. The girls he'd doublecrossed weren't important any more. Jonathan may have been a rogue, but he made being a rogue seem ... acceptable, the way every man of spirit ought to behave. At times I felt so bloody narrow-minded and dull in contrast.'

'You're not dull, and you never were!'

He grinned at her heated defence. 'Good, I hoped you'd say that.' Ahead lay a terrace of Victorian houses. Dan reduced speed and pulled the big car into the kerb. 'Pauline doesn't appear to be waving flags and eagerly awaiting your arrival,' he remarked as he cut the engine. 'Judging from the distinct lack of lights I'd say she isn't in.'

'She——' Jorja needed to clear her throat. 'She doesn't exactly know I'm coming.'

'I see.'

The phrase reeked with meaning, and so did the look she received. Her desire to avoid staying at the Old Vicarage had been declared as transparent as glass—and condemned.

'The key'll be under the plant pot as always,' she announced, trying to hit a note of unconcern. 'I'll just let myself in.'

Dan unclipped his seat belt. 'You'll let *us* in. I reckon as your chauffeur I deserve a cup of coffee, don't you? Besides, I am in the middle of explaining about Toby,' he reminded her, squashing flat any budding protests.

With misgivings, Jorja located the key and un-locked the door, letting them into the ground floor flat. She very much wanted to hear about Toby's paternity, but . . . She switched on the lights. So long as Dan restricted his talk to Toby, she was prepared to listen. However, the moment he moved on to other subjects, namely him and her, he would discover it was ejection time. Dan deposited her bags in the smaller of the two bedrooms, while she threw off her jacket and headed for the kitchen. Merrily described by Pauline as 'bijou', the yellow and white recess underwent a further shrinkage when her escort came to join her. Leaning against the wall, hands in his trouser pockets as he watched her, Dan was close, too close. Distracted by his presence, the preparation of two cups of instant coffee ballooned into a mammoth task. In the short time she had been away, Jorja had completely forgotten where the mugs were stacked, the position of the fridge, how to plug in the electric kettle.

'Carry on,' she prompted, conscious of bumping and barging around the place while she muddled through.

'Well, after a long run of being young, single and very free with his favours, Jonathan finally became engaged. My father went off into deliriums of delight. At last his prayers appeared to have been answered. Jon had committed himself to one woman, and a respectable type at that. My father was so relieved he decided he could be forgiven for past sins.'

'He always gives the impression of having doted on Jonathan,' she protested.

'He did. Whatever his faults, my brother was a charmer and Dad could be charmed as easily as anyone. Added to which, I suppose mixed in somewhere there had to be a sneaky admiration for his success with the ladies. Certainly my father's cronies were always digging him in the ribs and chuckling over the 'wild boy's' latest frolic. Sexist it may be, but many men would be proud if they sired a splendid stud like Jonathan.'

Jorja poured boiling water on to the coffee granules. 'Would you be proud?'

'No.' He took the mug she handed him and added a dash of milk. 'Especially not when I consider what's happened in consequence. I'll make damned certain Toby doesn't follow in his father's footsteps.' In the living-room he flung aside two of the fringed and tasselled scatter cushions to which Pauline was addicted, and sat himself down beside her on the well-worn settee. Pensively he frowned at the fireplace, where pelargoniums, pots of African violets and other flowering plants made a colourful display. 'Dad took it for granted, and so did I, that Jon's engagement meant he was ready to be faithful. We were forgetting a leopard doesn't change its spots. In no time at all he was splitting his time between Suzanne and Hilary. Two-timing par excellence!'

'Presumably Hilary knew he was engaged?'

'She did, but neither of them gave a damn. Her family had recently moved to Chester, so as far as Jonathan was concerned she was fresh meat. Regarding her motives——' Dan gave a derisive grunt. 'In addition to my brother's physical attractions, he was heir apparent to a thriving family firm. Hilary's background is modest, and she viewed him as quite a catch.' A mouthful of coffee was taken. 'Two days after the car crash, she appeared at the Old Vicarage. Being hospitalised, I missed the show, but to quote

my father she arrived in his study like a "refrigerator
on high heels". She coolly advised him that Jonathan
had made her pregnant, and that if he didn't want his
grandchild to be aborted he'd better think seriously
about making it worth her while.'

Jorja winced. 'God, how mercenary.'

His face had hardened into a mask. 'It was vintage
Hilary.'

There was a moment of silence.

'She must have been upset,' Jorja defended, not
quite knowing why. 'After all, she'd had the shock of
finding herself pregnant and then Jonathan's death.'

'She *didn't* find herself pregnant. Her condition had
been carefully contrived. Once, after the gin and
tonics had been flowing too readily, Hilary let me into
a secret. She admitted that although she'd assured Jon
she was taking precautions, she was doing nothing of
the sort. In fact, she'd even worked out the time when
she was most fertile and arranged an appropriate
pow-wow.' He snorted with disgust. 'If he'd known
he'd have been furious. I accept he was promiscuous,
but he wasn't completely irresponsible. He'd never
got a girl pregnant before.'

'Wasn't she playing a dangerous game, conceiving
a child by a man already committed elsewhere?'

'You forget her supreme self-confidence,' Dan
derided. 'If Hilary wants something to happen, she
does her damnedest to make it happen, and if others
receive shrapnel wounds in the process, so what?
Prior to Jonathan's death she'd apparently been all set
to usurp Suzanne. Given a little encouragement from
the child in her womb, she had no doubt she'd be the
one who'd make it down the aisle. Ironically, I'm

convinced that had he lived he'd have had no truck with her blackmail. Jon was enough of the heartless bastard to have thrust a bundle of notes in her direction and told her to make herself scarce.'

'It must have needed all Hilary's confidence to confront your father,' Jorja mused. 'How could she be sure he'd take her word for it that the child she was expecting *was* Jonathan's?'

'She couldn't, but my brother's lifestyle was such that he seemed more likely than not to be responsible.' Dan drained his mug and put it aside on a low tiled table. 'What Dad didn't know at the time was that Jon had already confessed to me that he was cheating Suzanne. He'd also made oblique references to him and Hilary being intimate, so when my father raised the issue later, I had to confirm the odds were on her telling the truth. From the start neither of us ever doubted the child was Jonathan's.'

'And you only need to look at Toby to see he's a Lecomber.'

'True.'

'But suppose your father had turned round and told her to go ahead with an abortion?'

Dan rubbed a long-fingered hand across his midriff, rumpling the charcoal grey sweatshirt. 'Remember I once said how Hilary has me weighed up?'

'To the last ounce,' Jorja confirmed.

'It's not just me. She might come across as the dizzy blonde, but she's remarkably shrewd where assessing her fellow men is concerned. She'd done her homework and taken note of everything Jonathan had said, because she knew all about my father's

distress over his lack of morals, how he'd been
pinning his hopes on the marriage to Suzanne
calming Jon down. She'd realised my father's a
respectable kind of person, that conformity matters to
him. Just as conformity matters to you,' Dan said as
an aside, and shot her a sharp-edged glance. 'Hilary
also knew how disappointed he was because both his
sons had managed to reach mid to late twenties
without providing a single grandchild. My father was
eager for the next generation of Lecombers.' Dan's
face, which had softened somewhat, now became a
stony mask again. 'Most people would have had some
compassion for a man whose elder son had just been
killed, whose second was on the critical list, but not
Hilary. That cruel bitch bowled in knowing full well
my father would be in deep shock, and thus
vulnerable. Full marks for a superb sense of timing!
The poor old devil had no alternative but to sit it out
and listen as she presented her ultimatum. He asked
for time to think it over, but the next day—boom! he
was felled by a massive coronary.'

Jorja frowned. Remnants of Dan's words on the
beach in Lanzarote were floating back to her. 'And
you believe the extra pressure Hilary put on him
helped cause it?' she questioned.

'She knew he was under tremendous strain, yet she
showed no mercy,' Dan bit out. 'I hold her responsible
in part. I always have. I always will,' he said, and fell
silent.

'At that point you'd have thought she would have
been tempted to forget the whole matter and go ahead
with—with an abortion,' Jorja suggested haltingly.

'Not her!' Fresh anger sparked him back to life.

'She waited until my father had been discharged from hospital, then promptly came a-calling again. By that time I was home and in full possession of the facts, so when she reappeared I made damn sure I was present. Hilary sailed in, "the refrigerator on high heels", and proceeded to spell it out that, owing to Dad inconsiderately wasting time by indulging in a heart attack, the opportunity to dispose of Jonathan's seed had been and gone.'

'Had it? Was she telling the truth?'

'Judging by Toby's birth date I doubt it, but I'm no expert on such things. Not that it mattered, because in the interim my father had decided that by hook or by crook his grandchild would survive.'

Jorja drank the last of her coffee, unconscious of the fact that it had gone cold. 'So he persuaded you to marry her?'

'Wait for it.' There was a strained smile. 'He offered to support Hilary during her pregnancy, provide a handsome cash settlement when the baby was born, and thereafter take steps to adopt it. Her attitude had already made it abundantly clear that the child, as a child, meant nothing to her. She was using it as a means of getting what she wanted—money.'

'But would the law allow an elderly man to adopt a child, even his own grandchild?'

'I've no idea, but again it didn't matter because we now discovered Hilary had stepped up her demands. She said she wasn't prepared for her child to be born on the wrong side of the sheets, and that I must marry her.' Dan shuddered, closing his eyes at the memory. 'God!' He shook his head in torment, then opened his eyes again. 'I told her the idea was preposterous, that

she had to be insane if she thought I'd shackle myself
to her in order to make amends for my brother
sleeping around. Jon had said she was no blushing
virgin, explained how *she'd* made the first approach,
so I knew fine this was extortion. I repeated how we'd
do the decent thing along the lines my father had
suggested, but as far as providing a husband went—
no way.'

'What was her reaction?' asked Jorja, when he
paused.

'She said in that case she was going to walk out of
the door, and cheerio! My father could go whistle as
far as his grandchild was concerned. She would
disappear abroad, give birth secretly and make
certain "father not known" was written on the birth
certificate. Then the baby would be offered for
adoption. I must admit I was so infuriated that I told
her to go ahead.' He let out a breath. 'Dad thought
otherwise. He pleaded with her to stay and talk
matters over.'

'One guess says Hilary deigned to agree?'

'After some beautifully acted refusals, yes. She
knew she had my father dangling on a string, that he
no more wanted Jonathan's child to be illegitimate
than she did, that he wouldn't be able to bear the
prospect of it growing up not knowing who its
antecedents were, and in an alien environment. In
time I calmed down, and——' Dan was back to
frowning at the plants in the fireplace. 'At that point
life had become alarmingly fragile. Jonathan, who
burst with vitality, was dead. My father appeared to
be only a heartbeat away from the grave. I'd almost
wound up as a cripple. This baby represented hope for

the future. A fresh start, if you like.'

'So you agreed to marry her?'

'Not then and there. I hedged around, trying to stave off a decision, trying desperately to come up with something, God knows what. Hilary became impatient. She flounced off saying she'd be back next morning for an answer, though she damn well knew what that answer was going to be. Then my father and I talked.'

'He began to apply the pressure?' Jorja queried.

'Yes. It's easy to understand why. At the time he feared his days were numbered. There seemed little chance of his surviving long enough to see me married, let alone a father. And here Jonathan's child was, ready and waiting. The fact that I'd recently broken off a relationship because the girl in question had started dropping heavy hints about engagement rings and so forth didn't help any. Dad took that to be a sign that I was destined for lifelong bachelorhood. When I protested I'd nothing against marriage, she'd just been the wrong girl, he refused to listen. He painted morose pictures of himself bereft of grandchildren, while all the time there was one out there somewhere; a child who'd bring him constant joy.'

'Which Toby does.'

'He's everything my father ever hoped for,' Dan agreed, massaging his midriff once more. 'As the day wore on so his agitation grew. Arguments were grabbed wherever he could find them. His face became pallid, he trembled, and I began to wonder if he might be heading for a second heart attack. To pacify him I agreed to consider Hilary's demand.' He gave a wry bark of laughter. 'That proved to be my undoing. Dad broke down and sobbed with gratitude. All he cared about was arranging for the child to be born bearing my name. With me as the father he believed we'd have some degree of control, that Hilary would no longer have us over a barrel. Little did we know!' He slid his hand beneath his sweatshirt to rub his bare flesh. 'Both of us took it for granted that once the baby was born she'd want to scoop up her ill-gotten gains, fix a divorce, and quit the scene, leaving the child behind. In retrospect we were unbelievably short-sighted.'

'When did you first realise Hilary intended to remain married?' asked Jorja, gazing at him in dismay.

'It must have been when Toby was around two months old. Right from the day she'd returned with him from the nursing home I'd been waiting for her to raise the subject of a divorce, and when she didn't I began to grow impatient. I told myself she was a tender new mother, that I must be sensitive and show restraint, though it was rapidly becoming clear that as tender new mothers went she was not going to win any prizes. A nanny had been engaged, and Hilary began disappearing for the day, most days. She spent her time exercising her figure back into shape, shopping for a brand-new wardrobe—my father insisted she be given a generous personal allowance in the hope of sweetening her—and drinking wine with her modelling friends. Toby was damn near forgotten. Eventually I reached the stage when I couldn't hold back any longer. I said it must be obvious I wanted a divorce, so how about it? But at the same time I took great care to emphasise that my father and I were no threat; that all Dad wanted was the opportunity to watch Toby grow and assist in his welfare. I offered to provide her with a house of her choice locally where she could live with her son or, if she preferred, she could have a house but leave Toby at the Old Vicarage with us.'

'That sounds reasonable.'

'I thought so. However, Hilary rejected the idea out of hand. She advised me that a divorce didn't figure in her scheme of things, and it was then that I realised living at the Old Vicarage must be some kind of status kick.'

'And being married to Daniel Lecomber?' Jorja suggested quietly.

'Maybe.' He was curt.

'But why did you leave it so long before you consulted a solicitor?'

He sighed. 'Because I knew my best chance, perhaps my only chance, of obtaining custody of Toby depended on Hilary also wanting a divorce. If she was seeking her freedom, she would be far more amenable. I pinned my hopes on her meeting someone else. When she started her jaunts abroad I kept thinking that any day it'd be—bingo!'

'Except that it wasn't, and for four years now you've been trapped into living a lie?'

'Yes, but——'

'Oh, Dan, that's dreadful!' An instinctive urge to give him comfort had Jorja placing her hand on his arm. To all outward appearances he was a properly married man with a son, when instead . . . A picture of him and Toby brought a lump to her throat. Dan poking the giggling three-year-old in his tummy and calling him 'Squidgebonks'. Seeing his love for the little boy, how could anyone ever guess he was not his father, merely his uncle? Her hand moved up to caress his cheek. 'One day you'll tell Toby the truth?' she asked.

'Yes, that's his essential right, though I'll wait until he's old enough to handle the information.' His brow creased. 'I wonder how he will handle it? Maybe he'll consider he's had a raw deal?'

'A raw deal with you as his father?' she protested. 'Never!'

'I'm only a surrogate, second best.'

'You're better for him than Jonathan would have been. Much better.' Jorja's hand moved round to the back of his neck, her fingers pushing into the thick pelt of fair hair. 'You are, Dan.'

He needed no encouragement to bend his head closer. 'Sweetheart, my brother was Superman. I'm mild-mannered Clark Kent.'

'Wrong way round!' she retorted.

'I don't think so.'

'I do. Jonathan was——' She wrinkled her nose in exasperation. 'But you're consistent, reliable. You can be trusted.' Enumerating his qualities while she gazed into the depths of his eyes caused a warmth. At first it stirred, then recklessly billowed. 'Make love to me, Dan,' she said. The words had not been consciously formed in her head, they just came out, surprising her as much as they obviously surprised him.

'Why?' He sounded cautious.

Jorja laughed delightedly. 'It's simple, because I love you. And you love me, don't you?'

'Yes.'

'Well then?'

He hesitated, until suddenly her gaiety, her certainty, her fever seemed to transfer themselves and Dan made a grab. There was a hungry moment of body against body, and then he was kissing her, holding her tight. Spontaneous combustion was the way he described it later. The kissing started with them sitting on the settee, then they were lying on it, then somehow they had slid off on to the floor. Dan did make some feeble protests, wondering about the wisdom of his undressing her here and now, groaning that she really shouldn't peel off his sweatshirt while they were still in the living-room, but they both became so infatuated with the exploration of each other's body that his words were lost. By the time he was urgently insisting they must go into a bedroom and on to a bed, they were both naked and clothes lay everywhere.

'Jorja, Jorja,' he sighed, madly involved with kissing her as he took her with him on to the nearest available mattress. He pulled her down, ravenously fondling. 'You have wonderful breasts, wonderful hips, wonderful, wonderful thighs.'

Those breasts and hips and thighs were caressed with his hands and with his mouth. Wantonly she lay beneath him, naked and open, succumbing with willing desperation to his fevered caresses, his eager kisses. Caresses and kisses which set her alight. Once, briefly, his hands ceased to fondle and the kisses stopped. Jorja reeled to the brink of despair. He could not refuse her now—not now, when her breasts were taut and straining, their tips a stretched fiery pink, not now when she was dewy with need. But Dan just wanted to look. And as his eyes moved over her, drinking in each alluring curve, each secret gulch, she sighed. His hands sought her body once more, stroking where his eyes had stroked, probing where his eyes had probed. He was a bold lover, demanding and returning pleasure in such outrageous amounts that Jorja sobbed, spiralling higher and yet higher into the realms of desire. Each particle of her body throbbed its pleasure, each nerve-end sang.

'I love you,' she whimpered, as he parted her thighs.

'And I love you,' he vowed, entering her.

Dan gripped her tight beneath him, and moved and moved and moved . . .

'Funny, I've never thought of Adam's apples as being sexy.' Jorja raised her head from his chest to smile. 'Yours is.'

'Does that mean you're about to jump on me again?' he asked, and the devilish look in his eyes made her heart beat out of rhythm.

'No.' She rubbed her cheek against the whorls of fair hair, enjoying their crispness, the way they tickled her skin. 'Not yet, anyhow.'

'Allow another five minutes and maybe you will?' Dan's arm tightened round her. 'Long live the liberated woman! I'm all for being carted off to bed while you have your way with me.'

'I don't normally act like this,' Jorja defended, feeling a trickle of dismay. What she had done, what they had done, was just beginning to filter through. 'I must have had a brainstorm. It's out of character for me to be so——'

'Rash?' he provided.

'Yes.' She pushed herself from him to sit up against the pillow. 'I don't know what happened.'

'For God's sake don't apologise. *Don't.*' Dan had stopped smiling. 'You made me feel ten feet tall. Okay, maybe asking me to make love to you wasn't what you intended, but it was spontaneous, Jorja. You didn't stop to think.'

'And that's good?' she asked doubtfully.

'Sometimes. If you perpetually pause to consider the pros and cons, you——' He broke off. 'Isn't that someone at the door?'

'Grief, it'll be Pauline!' She threw back the sheet and leapt out of bed. 'This is awful!'

'Is it?' He grinned lopsidedly. 'Pauline wasn't born yesterday. She must realise that——'

'Dan, get dressed. Please get dressed!'

He spread his arms. 'And what would you suggest I wear?'

'Grief!' she exclaimed a second time. Their clothes were strewn all over the living-room carpet. Jorja dashed to the door and peeped out, desperate for retrieval. 'Pauline?' she asked tentatively, then louder, 'Pauline?'

'Is that you, Jorja?' a distant voice enquired, and she let out a sigh of relief. Her friend was calling from beyond the front door. 'I saw Dan's Mercedes and thought it must be. I've forgotten my key and you've taken the one under the plant pot. Can you let me in?'

'Give me a minute,' she called, and began gathering up clothes right, left and centre, desperate to utilise this breathing space to good effect. 'Here,' she gasped. Dan was still in bed, so she dumped his share on top of him. 'Hurry, hurry!' she implored, and started to throw on her underwear.

'According to the books I've read and the films I've seen, the usual procedure after making love is to lie back and smoke, or exchange endearments in luxurious languor,' he drawled, rising to his feet. 'How come we're acting as though we're in a West End farce?' He pulled on his trousers, and as he closed the zip he chuckled. 'Jorja, all this panic is unnecessary.'

'It isn't!' She thrust his sweatshirt at him. She hurtled into the living-room, coming back with her shoes. 'And this isn't funny.'

'Have it your way, sweetheart.'

'What's taking so long?' yelled Pauline from the front door.

'I can't find the key,' Jorja called back. She spun round to Dan. 'Are you ready?' she hissed.

He stood up straight and clicked his heels. 'Manifestly decent, ma'am.'

'You don't need the key,' Pauline shouted. 'Just turn the snib.'

'I know—I remember. Sorry.' Simultaneously fastening her belt and tidying her hair, Jorja made for the hallway.

'I presume we're supposed to look as though we've just been playing bridge or something?' enquired an amused voice from behind. Dan was having great difficulty in keeping his face straight.

'Yes,' she snapped, flinging him a furious glance. She put on a wide, welcoming smile as she opened the front door. 'Hello, Pauline. I hope you don't mind my letting myself in, but I happened to be in Chester and

I knew you'd want me to stay with you, and Dan ran me over so I asked him in for a coffee, and——'

A large, tanned hand reached past her.

'Good evening, Pauline,' Dan grinned.

'Hello there,' smiled her friend. 'This is a nice surprise.'

'He's just leaving,' Jorja said hurriedly.

'I am?'

'You need to get back in case Toby wakes up.'

A blond brow was raised. 'Do I?'

'*Yes*!'

Why did he have to be so dense, so relaxed, so *happy*? For long enough Dan had argued against their becoming involved, but now that they had he did not appear in the least bit concerned.

'I guess having complied with your wishes once this evening, I shouldn't buck the system now,' he replied, shrugging good-natured shoulders. He beamed at Pauline. 'Goodnight.'

'Goodnight.' The redhead laughed. 'And on cue I'll disappear into the living-room, which will enable you two to say your own goodnights.'

'A girl with tact. I like that,' commented Dan as she departed. He got down to business. 'I'll pick you up tomorrow around eleven—okay?'

'Are you driving me back down to my father's?'

He nodded. 'But unfortunately I'll have to go there and back in the day. There's a meeting on Monday morning which I can't wriggle out of. Otherwise I'd stay over.' He gave her a teasing glance. 'If you'd have me.' He returned to business. 'If I pick you up at eleven and take you over to the Old Vicarage, you could spend some time with Toby again. Then we can have lunch, and head south early in the afternoon.'

'I ought to stay and eat with Pauline,' Jorja protested, feeling cornered. He was intent on strapping her into a straitjacket of organisation, when she needed time to think.

Dan looked past her out through the open door into the darkness, and sighed. 'When would you like me to collect you?' he enquired.

'Do we have to fix that now? Couldn't I ring you tomorrow?'

'All right, but don't leave it too late,' he replied, irritated by this refusal to make plans. 'It's a fair distance down to the Cotswolds.'

'Goodnight.'

She was anxious for him to leave. So many thoughts were swirling round inside her head, thoughts which needed to be sifted and examined. But how could that happen while Dan remained with her?

'Goodnight? Just goodnight?' His mouth spread into a grin. 'Is that it?' He put his arms round her.

'Someone might be watching,' she protested, aware that they were silhouetted in the hall.

'Let them watch.'

Her struggles lasted only a moment. Dan kissed her, and that meant surrender. Crushed beneath the sensual warmth of his mouth, her own parted. Her arms wound round his neck. The kiss, and those that followed, were deep and lingering, and when he finally released her Jorja was starry-eyed and all those swirling thoughts were cocooned in cotton wool.

'Goodnight, sweetheart,' he murmured.

'Goodnight,' she replied dreamily, watching as he strode down the path to his car and drove away.

'What was all that about?' Pauline giggled when she went inside.

Vaguely Jorja gazed around. 'I told you. He drove me here and——'

'And you invited Dan, Dan, the married man to come inside and have a cup of coffee?' the redhead teased, her eyebrows comically cocked. 'Whatever next?'

Dan, Dan, the married man. Jorja's vagueness vanished. The cotton wool fell from her thoughts. In chilling dismay, she pressed her knuckles hard against her teeth. What did it matter if his marriage was a lie? In the eyes of the world, in the eyes of the law, he was someone else's husband—and once again she had been an accomplice in adultery!

CHAPTER NINE

'MADE it!' panted Anne, reaching an open carriage door. She inspected her watch. 'And after all that rush you'll be amazed to hear there are now five whole minutes to spare.'

Jorja laughed as she heaved her suitcase and holdall on to the train. 'Thanks for stepping on the gas. I never realised you'd been trained as a racing driver!'

Her stepmother chuckled. 'I did break the speed limit once or twice, didn't I? But how could I let you be late on your first day at the Palisade?' Hands were pressed to hot cheeks. 'Fancy both of us sleeping in! With Monday being one of my free days I often catnap for a while after your father's gone to work, but this morning I went dead to the world. If the postman hadn't rung the bell I swear I'd be horizontal yet.'

'Ditto. It was three a.m. before I managed to drop off, but after that—clonk! If my alarm clock sounded, I never heard it.'

Anne gave her a hesitant look. 'I presume lying awake until the early hours is an indication that going to Chester didn't solve anything?'

The guard was approaching. Jorja climbed into the train, stood back as he slammed the door, then spoke through the open window.

'It cheered Toby up, as I explained last night.'

There was an exasperated sigh. 'That's not what I

meant. Seeing Dan didn't cheer *you* up?'

'No.'

'I wish I could do something to help, pet.'

'You can,' Jorja thrust.

'Refuse to reveal your whereabouts if he phones,' came the recital.

'*Please*!'

First voiced over their snatched breakfast, this request had been repeated in the car, and again as they had dashed up the slope to the railway station, yet each time Anne had come back with a protest.

'But don't you think——' she began, protesting once more.

'I can't explain, you'll just have to take my word that it *is* best if the two of us keep well away from each other,' Jorja insisted. The guard blew his whistle, and there came a jerk as the train slowly started to move. 'I went through hours of soul-searching last night, and although this isn't simply a matter of sticking up for my values, peace of mind and being able to live with myself are important. Guilt eats me up, I know from the past, and if Dan and I did . . . get together I'd feel guilty and it would ruin everything. But disregarding all that——' Jorja did not know if her message was making sense, but ploughed on, although Anne now needed to walk along the platform to remain within earshot. 'Disregarding all that,' she repeated, leaning out of the window, 'there are sound reasons why we're better off apart. For one, Hilary's attitude must be borne in mind. She's dangerous. She could——'

The older woman sighed. 'Okay.'

'You won't say I'm working at the Palisade?' Relief had brought a smile. 'Promise?'

'Promise.' No longer able to keep pace, Anne had to call.

Jorja lifted a hand and waved. 'Thanks. Thanks a million!'

She waved until her stepmother disappeared from sight, then picked up her luggage and went to find a seat. She knew Anne believed she was running away from a situation which should have been grabbed by the scruff of the neck and shaken, but Anne did not have access to all the facts. Given those, surely she must agree that separation was the only answer? Sightlessly Jorja stared out at the passing fields, her mind returning to the events of Saturday evening. Once again she had been the culprit. She should have had more sense, more control. But what about Dan's sense, his control? When she had asked him to make love to her, why hadn't he resisted? She had been relying on him to resist, she decided in a flash of perverse temper. And why his lack of remorse afterwards? He might have condemned Jonathan, yet there had been no reproach when he himself had broken the rules. But wasn't that the way of the world? Dan, like many others, would subscribe to the sexual discrimination which meant that when a man goes astray he's considered a bit of a lad, whereas if a woman does the same thing she runs the risk of being called a whore. Jorja went cold. A whore, was that what she was? There was no point in telling herself that if she explained how Dan's marriage was not a marriage, everyone would give them their blessing, because she could not explain. Hilary would fight against any disclosures, and fight dirty, but at the heart of the matter was the need for Toby's paternity to remain a secret. Visualising how Elsie *et al* would slaver over such a juicy morsel, she cringed. Silence was essential.

Yet wouldn't any explanation, given one were possible, at best be only a justification? Jorja had reached bare bones. Once the whys and wherefores had been stripped away, once the arguments, excuses, pleas in mitigation had been heard, the undeniable fact remained—she had made love with a married man. Technically she had done nothing wrong, in law Dan was named as the offender, yet the crime, like the tango, had taken two. The crime was adultery. She cringed again. Adul-ter-y. Adul-ter-y. The rhythm of the train took up the chant, and the word rattled round her head until she reached London.

The Palisade had a pretentious white facáde, coupled with a pretentious white and beige interior. The people, both staff and guests, seemed pretentious, too. Toffee-noses abounded. Long before the afternoon was halfway through, Jorja had begun to have doubts. Would she fit in here? Did she want to fit in? The man who interviewed her a month ago had been plump and pleasant and down-to-earth; she had liked him. Unfortunately in the interim he had received promotion and his place had been taken by Mr Higgins. Despite his name, Mr Higgins was the most toffee-nosed of the lot. Immaculate as a dummy from an expensive man's shop, and with the haughty air to match, he made sure of impressing his importance upon her.

'I enjoy a most favourable relationship with our clients,' he simpered, when she reported to his office at the end of the day. 'And I expect those in my department to emulate me.' Fastidiously he rearranged the peak of a scarlet handkerchief in his breast pocket. 'However, a word of caution—walk, don't run. All decisions must be referred to me. I find newcomers do show a tendency to be carried away. Even though you had a grounding in public relations work in the States, I imagine my predecessor most likely chose you for your looks,' he continued, pushing aside her *curriculum vitae* as though it carried a highly contagious disease. 'But please, no fraternising with male clients. Helpful, yes. Chummy, no. And as for your hair——'

'Yes?' Jorja was beginning to prickle. Not content with informing her that she was not what he himself would have selected, her new boss seemed all set to embark on more specific criticisms.

'It's pretty, but you must agree shoulder-length styles are somewhat antiquated. Likewise curls. A smoother, shorter cut would be more in keeping with the Palisade image.' With mean eyes, Mr Higgins scrutinised her. 'A bob, I think. Just below the ears. See to it, will you? There's no rush, weekend will suffice.' He consulted the clock on the wall. 'You may go now, Miss——?'

Her teeth grated together. 'Reynolds.'

'Quite so.'

Out in the corridor, Jorja glowered. Her hair was antiquated? He wanted it changed? How dare he! No other employer had ever found fault. Dan, for one, had liked her hair. Dan had *loved* it. Oh, Dan. She bowed her head. All through her initiation at the hotel her mind had persisted in straying to him, and now she wondered how he had reacted to Pauline's phone call on Sunday afternoon. Had he been angry when he had learned that she had already left Chester under her own steam? Had he felt she was panicking? Or had he understood her desperate need to get away— and accepted it? Maybe so. Dan had not chased after her, nor had he rung.

'Still here, Miss——?'

'Reynolds.'

Mr Higgins had emerged from his office, and now he frowned as though she was a vagrant he had found loitering on the premises.

'Quite so.' He gestured for her to accompany him towards the lobby. 'Have you found yourself a *pied-à-terre*?'

'Not yet. I did only arrive in London this morning.' Jorja thought how her immediate task must be to find a bed for the night. 'I'm looking for a guesthouse, to use as a base until permanent accommodation can be arranged. Could you recommend somewhere moderately priced?' she asked hopefully.

'So sorry, I know nothing about the cheaper end of the market,' he announced, and with that he left her.

'Quite so,' muttered Jorja.

She retrieved her luggage from the store, and struggled out through the revolving doors.

'Taxi, miss?' enquired the top-hatted doorman.

'No, thank you.'

Suitcase in one hand, holdall in the other, she retreated a few yards and dumped her load at the top of the flight of marble steps. With her holdall crammed to bulging point, it took a struggle to locate and then ease out her accommodation guide. In the train that morning Jorja had marked half a dozen of the more budget-wise guesthouses and, pushing her hair out of her eyes, she re-read the addresses. Where did she start? If only her knowledge of London wasn't so shaky. Kensington must be fairly close, but how about Maida Vale? A lost feeling crept over her. The rush-hour traffic was thundering past, the pavements were thronged with people, yet here she was, alone in this great big city. She could drop down dead, and nobody would give a damn. Stop it, she told herself. The first day in a new job is always strange, and if Mr Higgins isn't exactly welcoming, given time he could improve. Could he?

She leafed through the book. Did she head for Kensington, or was it to be Maida Vale? Kensington seemed the safer bet, so next she turned to a map of the Underground. By following the Piccadilly line, she could change——

Jorja glanced up. A car horn was being punched over and over again. Some fool had stopped dead-centre in the narrow road which serviced the hotel and in addition to making a heck of a racket was causing a hold-up.

'The gentleman appears to want you, miss,' called the commissionaire, using such a superior tone that she wondered if he might be Mr Higgins' brother.

She squinted down the steps. With the evening sun reflected in the windows, it was impossible to make out who was inside the car. To all intents and purposes the figure in the driving seat did appear to be waving in her direction, but who did she know in London?

'Not me,' she rejected firmly, and returned to

working out a route.

Jorja traced the map with a careful finger. First she must take the Piccadilly line, the one marked royal blue, and then change stations to continue on bright yellow, the Circle line. Was that the best way? With the car continuing to hoot, concentration was impossible, and she looked up and glared. The man was flapping his hand around like a lunatic. Hastily she lowered her eyes. He *was* waving at her. He must be trying to pick her up! Jorja went hot with embarrassment. The commissionaire was looking down his nose, and several passers-by had paused and appeared to be linking the commotion with her. Some very peculiar glances were coming her way. The glances intensified when the car window rolled down, and the man bellowed.

'Jorja!,

Her mouth dropped open. 'Dan?' she bleated.

She had recognised the car as a Mercedes, yet with Mercedes being ten a penny in London had made no connection. Now his fair head was clearly visible.

'Come on down here.'

Immediately the commissionaire stepped up, keen to expedite matters. 'May I assist with your luggage, miss?'

'Please.' She changed her mind. 'No, thank you.' If her instinct was to obey Dan's command, she was fast learning not to follow her instincts. Instincts equalled trouble. 'Could you tell me the way to the nearest tube station?' she enquired.

'Hurry up! There's a traffic jam behind me,' Dan shouted, gathering a fanfare of hoots from the traffic jam in question.

'Go. Just go.' Jorja motioned for him to move on, then turned back to the commissionaire. 'A tube station?' she demanded.

He pointed impatiently. Giving directions was one of his duties, but life would be easier all round if the silly girl would simply get into the Mercedes. Couldn't she see the havoc she was causing? Vehicles were building up at an alarming rate—already they were streaming back on to the main road.

'Right at the traffic lights, and about five hundred yards on the left you'll see——' His voice trailed to nothing. The driver had stormed from the car and was pounding up the steps, ready to give the girl a piece of his mind. Thank goodness. Now she would be made to go, and fast.

'I'd appreciate it if you could cut the chat and get a move on,' snapped Dan, as trapped drivers blasted a disgusted chorus at this extended delay.

'Why should I?' Her mixed-up feelings at seeing him at this unexpected time, in this unexpected place, fused into temper. 'You have no right to——'

'We'll discuss this in the car.' He frowned at the commissionaire. 'In private.'

'I'd rather discuss it now.' Although Dan had lifted her luggage, she stood firm. 'For a start we'll discuss how you knew where to find me. Anne's the traitor, isn't she? My God! This morning she promised to keep my whereabouts a secret and in less than eight hours she turns supergrass! I thought she was my friend. I thought I could rely on her. I thought she understood how——'

'I haven't been in touch with your stepmother,' he said irritably.

'Excuse me, sir,' began the commissionaire.

'Then who gave the game away?' enquired Jorja, her amber eyes ablaze with fury.

'You did.'

'I did not!'

'Excuse me, miss.'

'You told my father you were to work at a hotel which had recently opened near Hyde Park. Considering the damn place has been advertised on national television and featured in the Sunday supplements for months, I didn't need to be the brain of Britain to work out that it must be the Palisade.' He readjusted his grip on her luggage. 'Now, would you kindly oblige by following me and getting into the car?'

Jorja's anger had taken a nosedive. 'I'm—I'm not sure that's a good idea,' she said weakly.

'Get in the bloody car!'

With an on-off smile at the commissionaire, she skittered down the steps feeling well and truly squashed. She felt even worse when her entry into the Mercedes was greeted with catcalls and cheers from the drivers waiting behind. Dan slung her luggage into the boot, jumped in beside her, and they were off. Using a desperado's skill, he had them half a mile from the Palisade in what seemed like seconds. He cut, weaved and squeezed his way through the rush-hour traffic until they were thankfully anonymous.

Jorja cleared her throat. 'Could you take me to Kensington?' she enquired, needing to show some kind of initiative. Throughout all this she had been clutching the accommodation guide, and she rapidly found the page.

'No,' he said, when she began to read out the

address. He had coated the word in ground glass. 'The only place I'm taking you is Chester.'

'But I can't go there!' she wailed, noticing with dismay how he had swung the Mercedes left on to a lane of the highway marked 'The North' in big white letters. 'I have to be back at the Palisade by nine tomorrow morning!'

'To hell with the Palisade!' he barked.

'Be reasonable, Dan. You must see I can't just . . . walk out on them.'

'Why not? You've walked out on me—*twice*.'

'That was different,' Jorja muttered uncomfortably.

'Very different. Your commitment to that hotel amounts to one afternoon, whereas you've known me most of your life, worked with me for months, loved me for damn near as long. You may not have realised it, but you did,' he snapped, when she started up with protests. 'However, your days of walking out on me are over, lady! In future——'

'We don't have a future.' The past five minutes had seen Jorja rocketing around between being angry, to feeling squashed, to being uncomfortable. Now she was weepy and wistful. 'As long as you're Hilary's husband——'

'You like Italian food, don't you?' he cut in.

'Er—yes.'

'Fine, we'll stop here.' He gestured ahead towards a modern terrace, on the end of which was a glass-fronted restaurant. In splendid gold scrolled letters, a sign announced 'Pieroni's'. 'I'm famished. I didn't have time for lunch because straight after I finished my meeting I drove down here. I'm sorry if it's on the early side for dinner for you, but there is a lengthy journey ahead of us.' He swung into a side street and parked, but before Jorja could summon up the strength to climb out he placed his fingers on her wrist. 'We do have a future, sweetheart.'

'No.' Her weepiness had become a blur of tears. 'Dan, our joining forces, even discreetly, is wrong. You're married and——'

'I'm not married,' he said softly. 'Not any longer. You see, on Saturday morning I became the proud owner of a decree absolute. It's tucked up in the safe at home—I'll show it to you when we arrive.'

Jorja gazed at him. She felt as if she was in a trance. 'Say that again.'

'Hilary has gone for good. The divorce is final.' He gave a wide smile. 'I'm a free man.'

'The divorce has gone—gone through?' she stammered. 'And you knew on Saturday?'

'I did.'

'Yet you never told me?' Her voice rose in pitch. 'You kept quiet and let me believe we'd—we'd committed adultery!'

Dan stroked her wrist. 'Sweetheart, I didn't mean it to be like that, but somehow things snowballed.'

She snatched her hand away. 'I've been through agony!'

'It's over now.'

'You mean I'm expected to forgive and forget? No way!' It was an hysterical assertion. Too much had happened too quickly, and having been the round of so many other emotions, Jorja had returned to anger. 'We were together for—I don't know how many hours on Saturday, and you never said a word? What kind of a game is that?' she demanded.

'No game.' Dan's calm contrasted with her flushed-faced fury. 'And as far as not saying a word's concerned, you must agree you didn't give me much chance. Just as you're not giving me much chance now.' He raised an index finger to her mouth. 'Button it.' Jorja glared, but when his finger fell away she remained silent. 'If you think back you'll recall that every time I attempted to take a hand in directing the conversation you jumped in with a diversion.'

'How was I to know you wanted to tell me you were divorced?'

'Impossible. But you know now.'

'You *could* have said something,' she muttered.

'I could.' Dan twisted in his seat to face her. 'Give me a chance to explain what's been happening these past months, and then maybe you won't be so hard on me. Remember how we returned from Lanzarote and Hilary was there to greet us with the news that she wanted to rearrange the divorce?'

'I do,' said Jorja, with feeling.

'We both jumped to the wrong conclusion. It turned out she didn't want to delay things, she wanted to speed them up. Scaring the life out of me was her idea of a joke. She has,' he said drily, 'a somewhat cruel sense of humour.'

'Why did she want to speed things up?'

'Because she had a highly desirable second husband organised, a German called Manfred Gruber.'

'Not one of the steel Grubers?'

'Son and heir to the founding father, no less.' He grinned at her astonishment. 'The wealth Gruber has access to must make my worldly possessions seem like chickenfeed, but I'll fill you in on him later. The crux is that when Hilary requested an acceleration, it seemed too good to be true. In the past she's been so consistently devious that although she talkcd about a guy who wanted to marry her, I couldn't believe it wasn't some kind of a stunt she was pulling. Even when she engaged a local solicitor to push through the various procedures on her behalf, I expected the bottom to drop out at any minute. That's why I didn't tell either you or my father what was going on. There seemed no point building up false hopes.'

'A hint wouldn't have hurt,' Jorja chided.

'Even a hint would have meant you going through hell. Believe me, I know. The closer the time came to the issue of the first decree, the more anxious I grew. Even when it came through I kept reminding myself there were still six weeks to go, six weeks in which Hilary could do an abrupt about-turn.' Dan reached for her hand. 'Also by that time an element of superstition had entered into things. I'd not said a word to anyone and everything had gone fine, so speaking out smacked of tempting fate. I couldn't risk it.'

'By everything going fine, I take it you mean you've obtained custody of Toby?'

'Complete custody and control. Hilary agreed to every single thing I requested, and she didn't claim alimony! When my solicitor handed over the first decree he commented on how smoothly the divorce was proceeding, but—' Dan pulled down his mouth '—as smooth isn't a word you associate with Hilary, I continued to sweat it out. Last Saturday, as I was preparing to drive down and see you, the phone rang.

It was her solicitor, asking me to go and see him. He said the matter was urgent.' He let out a hiss of tortured remembrance. 'Before I had the wit to ask for details, he'd rung off, so in the time it took to reach his office I'd managed to list a hundred and one reasons for Hilary pulling the plug. When I staggered into his presence, I was a nervous wreck! He calmly handed me an envelope and inside was the decree absolute. Don't ask me how, but Gruber had pulled strings and the final papers had gone through quicker than expected. Gruber had insisted on Hilary's solicitor giving me the decree in person, because he wanted to make sure everything was cut and dried.' He laughed. 'I was so damn pleased I almost foxtrotted the guy round his office. Then I sped home, happily planning the special moment when I'd break the news to you.'

'Why not announce it when I arrived with your father?' asked Jorja.

'Because I didn't want to share the news three-way, not initially. It had to be just between me and you. Call that selfish, but love is selfish. I'd presumed you'd be spending the night at the Old Vicarage, so I pictured us alone together in the lamplight when my father had gone to bed. I was going to tell you I was free, you were going to fall into my arms.' Dan raised his eyebrows. 'Etc., etc. Then it turned out you had a mule-stubborn idea about staying at Pauline's.'

'I had to, Dan. I knew I couldn't trust——'

'Me?' he cut in.

Jorja gave a sheepish grin. 'No, me.'

'You were deliciously eager on Saturday,' he said, and raised her hand to his lips. He kissed her fingertips one by one. 'However, to continue. Then I decided I'd tell you in the car, but that didn't work out because we became involved in talking about Toby. Next thing I knew, you were demanding I make love to you!'

'Why didn't you tell me then?'

'It would seem to have been the ideal moment,' Dan agreed slowly, 'but as the opportunities to explain vanished one after another, I reached the decision to keep quiet.'

'Why?' she asked, intrigued.

He sucked in his lower lip. 'A number of reasons. They were all mixed up at the time, but coming down in the car I started to sort them out. One was that we'd just been talking about Jonathan, and it was in my head how you'd fallen for him. I know you said I was Superman, not him, but I still wondered——' Dan shifted in his seat. 'This sounds crazy, but it's how I felt. It seemed that if we made love without the carrot of marriage dangling in front of your nose you were giving me extra proof that you loved me. *Me*, Jorja. I needed to be sure there wasn't any residual feeling for my brother left inside you.'

She looked at him, her eyes wide. 'I never fell for Jonathan. To be frank, I didn't even like him very much.'

'You went out on dates with him,' Dan protested.

'Five times, that's all.'

'There'd have been more if—' he frowned '—if Jonathan hadn't discarded you.'

'Wrong! It was the other way round, I discarded him.'

'Not according to Jon.'

'You think he'd have freely admitted to being dumped?'

'No, I suppose not,' he agreed.

'I understood you were famished?' she said, when he lapsed into silence.

'I am.' Dan roused himself. 'Shall we go?'

His random choice proved to be a good one. Pieroni's had a walled garden at the rear where tables and chairs were set out on a paved terrace, and it was here the waiter guided them. With roses blooming all around, the evening air was fragrant. They sat beneath a large white fringed umberella and studied the menu.

'I don't understand why you went out with my brother if you didn't particularly like him,' said Dan, when their orders had been taken and a carafe of wine provided.

'For a bet.'

'Jonathan wouldn't have been very flattered!'

Jorja grinned. 'I can't help that. It was the last few weeks at school after the examinations,' she explained, 'and a group of us had time to kill. As often happens when teenage girls get together, the conversation turned to the opposite sex. Tania, a friend of mine, went on at great length about how dreamy Jonathan was. She reckoned the highlight of her life would be if he asked her out, but he wouldn't because she was too young. She said he'd never give a schoolgirl a second glance. I didn't agree. I said he'd go out with anything in skirts so long as it was reasonably pretty.'

Dan sighed. 'I guess you were right.'

'A long argument followed, and at the end Tania

and the four other girls in the group each bet me a pound I couldn't get myself a date with him.'

'Five pounds equalled five dates?'

She nodded. 'It was a challenge I couldn't refuse.'

'So how did you get Jonathan interested?' he enquired, taking a mouthful of wine.

'I appeared at the rugby club the next Saturday, stood on the touchline, and every time he galloped past I fluttered my eyelashes.'

'As you did with Lorenzo?' he asked drily.

Jorja laughed. 'Yes, and it worked.' The waiter came up with their order, lasagne for her, cannelloni for Dan, and she waited until they had been served before continuing. 'The dates were nothing special. I found him—okay, charming, but too high-powered. Nothing clicked.'

'Something must have clicked with Jonathan,' he protested. 'He did take you out five times. What was his reaction when you said goodbye?' he asked, when she shrugged.

'He protested, and at great length. The novelty of being dumped wasn't one he appeared to enjoy. For a couple of weeks he was constantly on the telephone, then I presume he met someone new, because the phone calls stopped and I never heard from him again.'

'You sneaked off to a hidey-hole with your five pounds and gloated?'

'I did.' Jorja took a forkful of pasta. 'Mmm, lovely,' she smiled, and for a few minutes they ate in silence. 'You mentioned other reasons for deciding to keep quiet about your divorce. What were they?'

Dan moved a piece of cannelloni around his plate.

'Sweetheart, like anyone else I'm riddled with insecurities. If we made love without your knowing I was free it seemed as if it genuinely, I mean *not at all*, didn't matter that—' he stopped scowling down at his plate and met her eyes point-blank, '—that I have a handicap. Hell, I know a man who limps doesn't exactly give off a macho image, and——'

'If you think I give a damn about your limp, Daniel Lecomber, you're nuts!'

'Am I?'

'Yes!'

He blinked. 'Oh.'

'Any other skittles I can knock down?' she asked, with a grin.

'Yes.' There was a long pause. 'The third, and last, reason why I wanted to leave you in ignorance arose from ... perversity, I guess.' He frowned, trying to find the right words to express himself. 'You'd always been so violently anti getting involved on the grounds I was married. I accept it was the right way to behave,' he continued quickly, 'but you came at me with such an intense distrust mechanism. When you saw me you refused to see a friend, someone who cared for you and who needed your care. All you saw was my marital status. But by giving yourself to me on Saturday, you sacrificed that distrust in the name of love. Ethically it may not have been right, emotionally it was.' He gave a lopsided grin. 'Are you on my wavelength?'

'I am, and you're right. I did overreact. I never meant to come on so strong, and I never meant to hurt you, Dan, but——' Jorja took a deep breath. 'When I was in Australia I met a man called Mark.' She put down her fork. 'Now it's my turn to do some explaining.'

She told him everything. How she had fallen in love, how she had been hoodwinked, about Mae and the children appearing, about the sickening sense of shame which she had carried about with her ever since. Pasta plates had been cleared, desserts eaten, and they were drinking coffee by the time her account ended.

'I came home swearing I'd never be put in that position again, and to protect myself I carried a little slogan round in my head—beware of married men.'

Dan reached across the table, covering her hand with his own.

'Then how do you feel about being the wife of one? And I am proposing.'

'I think I'd like it. I think I'd love it. Yes, I will marry you,' she adjusted, when he tipped his chair forward and kissed her over the coffee cups.

'*Mama mia*!' shrugged the waiter, who had arrived with a fresh pot. He left them alone to gaze into each other's eyes and murmur, then returned to the task ten minutes later.

'Where did Hilary find this Manfred Gruber?' Jorja asked, when her cup had been refilled and she had one foot back on earth, if not two.

'In the south of France. Her stories of so much modelling work had never rung true, so it was no suprise to learn that she'd spent more time with him than before the camera.' Dan chuckled. 'I get the impression she was required to pull out all the stops before she finally managed to tie him down.'

'But now it's mink coats and limousines all the way?'

'Probably, yet even if Gruber does have a reputation for being something of a playboy he's not as easy-going as you'd imagine. A marriage contract has been drawn up, one which sounds heavily weighted on his side. What belongs to Gruber obviously stays with Gruber, because one of the clauses is about Hilary more or less disowning Toby. Gruber has no objection to her and their offspring enjoying his wealth, but he intends to ensure that no one outside the family should ever be in a position to make claim. Naturally Hilary's so eager to bag herself a millionaire that she'll agree to anything.'

'Even to turning her back on her own son!' Jorja snorted disgustedly.

'She's been doing that for the past three years,' Dan pointed out. 'She insisted there must be no contact between them from now on, and I see no reason to disbelieve her.'

'When does she marry Gruber?'

'Next week. It's his thirty-sixth birthday, and he thinks it'd be fun to get hitched then. Fun!' Dan stole a cube from the sugar bowl, popped it in to his mouth and munched. 'Isn't it bloody marvellous? Here I've been fighting to negotiate my freedom for nigh on four interminable years, and finally I'm rushed along so some guy can blow out his candles and cut a wedding cake all on the same day!'

Jorja gave a laughing shrug, then sobered. 'Did Hilary come and say a proper goodbye to Toby?'

He grunted. 'I wouldn't call it proper! Some clothes needed to be collected, so she took the opportunity to combine the two tasks. The clothes warranted more than an hour of her time, her son was spared five minutes.' A pulse had begun to throb in Dan's temple. 'When I think of how that callous bitch left him—God!' He took a moment to collect himself. 'She was wearing a pale brocade suit, which meant she couldn't risk grubby little hands getting too close. She just stood in the hall, and said she was sorry but she wouldn't be able to come and see him again. There were no cuddles, no kisses. Damn all!'

'Oh, Dan!' Jorja reached for his hand. 'What did Toby do?'

'Looked at her. Poor kid didn't have a clue what she was talking about. Then Hilary remembered a jacket she'd left in a wardrobe and she disappeared upstairs. He went off to ride on his trike. End of story.' Dan gave a curt laugh. 'At least there's the satisfaction of knowing that if she doesn't miss him, he isn't going to miss her.'

Jorja nodded, then she recalled the blonde's antics at his office. 'But will Hilary miss you?' she asked quietly.

'Me?'

'Don't play the big innocent. I know very well she—lusted after you.' Her head was tilted, and she was smiling. 'How did Hilary behave on your wedding day? Did she pretend it was a real love match?'

Dan groaned. 'She did.'

'I thought she might have done. And?' Jorja prompted.

'It threw me completely. She held on to my arm, gazed up as if she was an adoring bride. The few folk who were there went away convinced she was dotty about me. The whole day was a mockery.' He shuddered. 'I get goose-pimples when I think about it.'

'And did you have a happy honeymoon?' Jorja enquired lightly.

'Give me a break! After the ceremony we went back to the Old Vicarage, and our separate rooms.'

'To live in splendid isolation?'

There was an infinitesimal pause. 'Yes.

'Come clean, Dan.'

He saw her twinkle of amusement. 'Okay, Hilary made advances,' he admitted.

'She raped you on your wedding night?'

'Not quite. She waited a week, then I emerged from the shower one night to find her sitting up in my bed wearing a see-through nightdress and a sexy pose. I couldn't believe it. Here was a woman who'd forced me into marrying her, and who was now suggesting that as we'd made the trip to the registrar's we might well have some mileage out of it. I was . . . outraged!'

'You showed her the door?'

'I slung her out of it!'

'Perhaps she was hoping you'd fall in love with her?' Jorja's twinkle had become a grin. 'You are rather sexy and gorgeous.'

'All Hilary wanted was a bedmate. Any male would have suited. I just happened to be around.'

'You're too modest!'

'And you're too biased,' Dan responded.

'Were any other seductions attempted?'

'Occasionally over the years, but that's one area where she totally misjudged me.'

'You wouldn't be wooed?'

'Like hell!' he blasted, then saw her grin. 'Like hell,' he repeated, on a more moderate level. 'But you can woo me any time. How about tonight? And don't think you can forestall me by rushing off to Pauline's. You're staying at the Old Vicarage. Understand?'

'Yes, Dan.' She was appropriately meek. 'In your room?'

'For my father's sake it had better be along the corridor. But you can be sure of one thing, when you hear the patter of tiny feet they won't be Toby's!'

In contrast to Saturday's northbound journey with his Dan's father, this trip was one long conversation. So much needed to be discussed. When they married. Where they married. And how about a honeymoon?

'I know the perfect place,' Dan grinned. 'It's an apartment in Lanzarote, number 56.' Jorja thumped him on the knee, and in the ensuing rumpus he decided he might possibly be persuaded to change that to the Seychelles. 'I'm tempted to hand Sally over to Bruce and ask you to come back to the office,' he said, once order had been restored. 'But I must confess I'd rather you devoted your energies to being my wife than my P.A. Besides—' he didn't thump her knee, he squeezed it '—we don't want to leave it too long before Toby has a playmate, do we?'

When they reached the Old Vicarage, the conversation continued. Mr Lecomber had been advised of his son's divorce, but now needed to be given full details of his marriage. There were congratulations and celebratory drinks, and somehow the old man steered the conversation round his way.

'I shall find myself a bungalow and leave you in peace,' he declared happily. 'I've noticed a most attractive one on our books. It has two bedrooms—I need a spare one for when Toby comes to stay—and a dining-kitchen and——'

Midnight was long gone before Jorja was installed in the spare room, but it was only a matter of minutes before she heard the patter of feet.

'I'm not even properly undressed yet,' she protested, laughing as Dan flung off his dressing-gown and reached for her.

'Then I'll help—improperly.'

Her bra was unfastened, and warm hands took the place of white satin as support. 'Beautiful,' he murmured, stroking the smooth, smooth undersides. He kissed her. 'Beautiful.'

As his fingers tugged the rosy knubs into a sensual tightness, Jorja whimpered, and when his mouth covered where his fingers had been, her whimpers became throaty moans of pleasure. Next her panties were slid from her hips, and once again she felt his touch. She cried out softly. He kissed her again.

'Touch me,' Dan begged, and when she moved her hand she felt his body throb, shudder, and fiercely seek control.

He was kissing her again, his tongue in her mouth, his breath mixed with her breath, while his hands were gently exploring. In time his breathing became ragged, his need paramount. His touch changed, and there was a moment when Jorja could not keep pace. Then Dan banked down his passion, and as his fingers stroked, his mouth sucked and caressed, her heat billowed to equal his. Whatever he wanted, she wanted, and she blossomed. Saying something between gritted teeth, Dan thrust into her. Out and in again. Another muttered word. A declaration of his love. Forever. Another thrust. Jorja clung and sobbed, carving her fingernails across the width of his back.

'Darling Dan!'

'Sweetheart!' he groaned.

The final fetters of control snapped, and they plunged headlong into that giddy, whirling abyss called fulfilment.

In the name of respectability, Dan had intended to return to his own room in time for the household waking up—but it did not happen that way. They spent the night interlocked and interlocking, and although he did manage to awaken when the sky grew light, the temptation of the curvy, sleep-soft body next to his proved too great. They made love again, then wallowed in the luxurious languor Dan had read about in books and seen in films. In real life it was, he declared, so much more satisfying.

'Uh, uh,' he murmured, when there was a noise on the landing. 'Hear those tiny feet? Now those are Toby's.'

'Daddy?' The little boy had found his room empty. 'Where my daddy?'

'In here,' called Dan, hearing the note of panic. He kissed Jorja on the brow. 'Sorry, sweetheart, we've been caught. Not exactly in the act, but near enough.'

The door was pushed open and a small figure in

pale blue pyjamas bounded into the room. He stopped in surprise. 'Jorja!' he exclaimed, and laughed delightedly. With complete disregard for Dan's finer feelings, he jumped on to the bed and crawled over him to get at her. 'You come to see me?' he asked, wriggling down, making a space for himself between them which he knew had been especially reserved.

She kissed the top of his head. 'Yes, I've come to see you.'

The three-year-old bedded himself in. 'Do you love me?' he demanded.

'I do.'

'How much?'

'Oodles and oodles,' she vowed.

Dan rolled weary grey eyes to the ceiling. 'My God, we've still to tie the knot, and already I've been superseded by a newer model! Maybe not quite,' he amended, when she touched him under the bedclothes.

Toby looked from one smiling face to the other. He knew something was happening, but could not decide what. He needed to plonk his hand on Jorja's chin before he got her attention.

'And do you love my daddy?'

It was a risky question, he knew, but one which he needed to ask. His small face puckered as he waited for her answer.

'Yes, I do.'

Giggling, the little boy wriggled down further, enjoying a cosy moment of bliss. She loved his daddy! Everything was going to be all right.

'How much?'

'How much do you think?'

'Oodles and oodles?'

Jorja smiled at the man on the other pillow, a man whose eyes were soft with love.

'*And* oodles,' she said.

Harlequin Presents

Coming Next Month

Available in October wherever paperback books are sold, or through Harlequin Reader Service:

In the U.S.
901 Fuhrmann Blvd.
P.O. Box 1397
Buffalo, N.Y. 14240-1397

In Canada
P.O. Box 603
Fort Erie, Ontario
L2A 5X3

An enticing new historical romance!

Spring Will Come

SHERRY DeBorde

It was 1852, and the steamy South was in its last hours of gentility. Camille Braxton Beaufort went searching for the one man she knew she could trust, and under his protection had her first lesson in love....

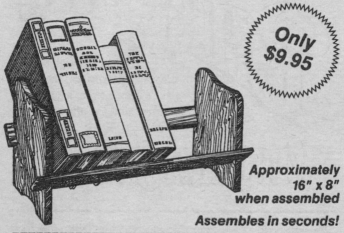

It was a misunderstanding that could cost a young woman her virtue, and a notorious rake his heart.

THE BARGAIN

When Ashleigh Sinclair
arrives at Ravensford, she thinks
she's been hired as a governess,
but Lord Brett Westmont has other ideas....

VERONICA SATTLER

**For the millions who can't read
Give the Gift of Literacy**

One out of five adults in North America
cannot read or write well enough
to fill out a job application
or understand the directions on a bottle of medicine.

You can change all this by joining the fight
against illiteracy.

For more information write to:
Contact, Box 81826, Lincoln, Neb. 68501
In the United States, call toll free: 1-800-228-8813

**The only degree you need
is a degree of caring**

LIT-A-1R